Tenterhooks

Claire-Lise Kieffer is Franco-German and lives in Galway. Her fiction has appeared in the literary journals *Banshee, Profiles, Crossways* and *The Honest Ulsterman*, among others. She was a recipient of the Arts Council Agility Award in 2022 and 2024 and is working on a novel.

Tenterhooks

Claire-Lise Kieffer

BANSHEE PRESS

First published 2025 by Banshee Press
www.bansheepress.org

A CIP record for this title is available from the British Library.

the arts council **funding**
chomhairle
ealaíon **literature** Banshee Press gratefully acknowledges
the financial assistance of the Arts Council.

ISBN 978-1-7393979-6-8

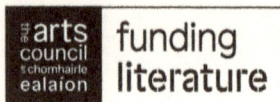

Versions of these stories previously appeared in the following: 'The
New Irish' in *Bending Genres*; 'Marmite' in *Banshee*; 'Saturday Night
Dinner' in *Crossways*; 'Woodlice Lessons' in *Books Ireland*; 'A Life Well
Lived' in *Amsterdam Quarterly*; 'Galway Sinking' in *Seaborne*

Set in Palatino by Eimear Ryan
Cover design by Jack Smyth
Printed and bound in Great Britain by Clays Ltd, Elcograf S.p.A.

For Hélène and Anne

Contents

Tenterhooks

The stubble on the boy's head mimics the grass on the sloping green: a two on the sides, six on top, for biodiversity. Galway has her back turned to him, the cathedral, the hospital, the houses all facing towards the sea. He is a black cut-out against the carpet of city lights, the Clifton Hill reservoir behind him.

He ambles down to the footpath and his trained eye catches on an empty naggin of vodka. He recognizes the blue label, the way the glass is smashed flat into the tarmac so it looks like an imprint of a naggin. He looks for and finds the plastic MiWadi, still half-full of purple liquid, a few steps further in the bushes.

During his one holiday abroad, camping in the south of France, the boy had found dead toads on the road. Their homing instinct drove them back to old mating grounds, rivers bracketed by holiday traffic. By the time he found them, they were flat and dry and could be flipped over like pancakes.

He follows the trail towards home. At the next streetlight, another blue label holds together jagged diamonds in the same way his mother holds together their burst family. The boy's older sisters – Katie Mary Farrah Shauna, a litany of girls – have all left the house. Katie's in Australia, Mary had the abortion, and Farrah and Shauna are in nursing school in Limerick. He stands still, listening, but Carraig Liath estate is silent. Only the restless hum of town floats up on wings of turf, peppered with police sirens.

At the worksite, he stops to look at the sleeping metal beasts fenced in for the night. He has not yet lost a small boy's fascination for large machines. With their oversized jackhammers and dinosaurian shovels, they have erupted the street, laid bare its vital organs. On the fence, a sign shows a picture of a corroded pipe next to a picture of a brand-new pipe, sexy as a pipe can be. 'National Leakage Reduction Programme', reads the heading. The inhabitants of Carraig Liath are that thick, they need to be told what's good for them. The hammering has been going on for weeks, getting on people's nerves. You can trace the tarmacked scar from where it starts down at the Siobhan McKenna Road, runs past Laurel Stores and up the first green. The boy turns his head and sees his house, and the disheartening bright patch on the drive that means the kitchen light is on.

Instead of going in the front door, he picks his steps around the back of the house. He inches one of the bins against the wall, pulls up a knee and then the other, and stands on the wobbly lid with a trapeze artist's balance. He grabs onto the first-floor windowsill, tenses his young muscles and drags himself up and in, rolling onto his bed. Again, he freezes into stillness. The drone of his father's voice, coming up from the kitchen, has not changed its tempo. It has the muffled and enervating quality of a mosquito by your ear at night. The boy sits up and thinks of locking his door, but remembers he no longer has the key. He could open it and listen to his father's words, but he doesn't, has long since stopped trying to understand what eats him.

*

The boy's father, Garda Sergeant Jimmy Cassidy, looks drained and flabby to his wife when he sits up in the following morning's reproachful light. Toothpick legs angle out of Calvin Klein boxers, and the pink sausages of his gut nestle under sparse grey vegetation. He no longer works out to keep the flesh on his limbs and off his midriff. And yet, thinks Cora Cassidy, he still has the fallen angel face, the heart-wrenching bend in the nose where it was broken, those sharp cowboy features for which a girl would set herself on fire. He cradles his beautiful head in aristocratic hands – where did he get those hands, and he a farmer's son? – as though trying to keep the hammering out, and even now, morning desire spreads in her like ink. The vodka is beating him from the inside out, the sound of the hydraulic concrete breaker down at the worksite, from the outside in.

'They're fucking at it again,' he whimpers, a boyish complaint in which she can hear their son. He turns and catches her looking at him with what he calls 'doggy eyes'. 'How bout some breakfast,' he says in his hard voice. He unfolds a once-elegant frame and makes for the bathroom. Cora welcomes in an uncharitable thought: funny how his gut looks like a permanent pregnancy, fourth or fifth month, solid.

The kitchen is lined with damp, bloated wallpaper that has absorbed thirty years' worth of cabbage and bacon stew. The pastel pink roses seemed like a cheerful pattern at the time. Now the roses have rotted into a poisonous purple and the ghosts of dinners past threaten to burst out at every meal. There is never the time nor the money for a new wall.

The man and the boy ladle porridge into themselves in silence. They stare at each other with the same bad look, never letting the other out of sight, like wolves. Why do they have to be that way? When the boy is halfway through his bowl, Cora puts a hand on his arm:

'Why don't you go up, pack your bag for school.'

The boy stands without saying anything, waits.

'Hold on,' Jimmy says.

'Jimmy,' Cora says.

'Where were you last night?'

'None of your fucking business.'

'You little shit!' Jimmy has jumped up; the kitchen chair clatters to the ground.

'Why do you always have to needle your dad so.' Warm morning tears bathe Cora's face. She can't remember a morning without tears. It's at that stage where she starts bawling Pavlovian porridge tears as soon as she puts the pot on.

Thirteen years ago, when the boy was born, everything seemed to take a turn for the worse. She can't help but think sometimes that this boy is some sort of retribution, some way of saying they should have stopped after the fourth girl, instead of trying for a boy so much later, Jimmy's obsession. She hears the doctor's disapproving tone at the check-up: 'I did warn you about the risk of prolapse after the last one, Mrs Cassidy,' a message from hell or heaven, her little Satan.

'Shove it, Cora,' says the boy in a tone so perfectly imitating his father's that she really does stop crying, out of shock.

'Don't talk to your mother that way!' Jimmy roars. No, thinks Cora, that's *your* prerogative. 'Where in the name of fuck is my belt?' He hasn't needed to wear a belt in a while thanks to his sloping morphology, but he keeps one on hand for occasions just like this. The boy says as much. What he says is:

8

'You don't need one, lardass.'

It's not true that all unhappy families are unhappy in their own way, that's just something they say to make themselves feel better, to feel special, to have a good reason for being unhappy.

Jimmy follows the road shoelacing down Carraig Liath. He sits up high in his white Volvo with the 'Pro-Life & Proud' sticker on its rear. A foreigner visiting Carraig Liath for the first time might mistake these blood-red stickers for parking permits, so ubiquitous are they in the estate. The people who live here, at the very edge of Galway City, last stop before the bog, are country people who moved to the city. The country clings to them like sods of turf cling to the soles of work boots, and their beliefs are exacerbated by expatriation.

After the first curve, Jimmy brakes for a front-load truck crossing with a bellyful of gravel. The lad at the wheel gives him a two-finger salute and Jimmy's two fingers automatically straighten in response. Behind the fence, machines move stone and dirt around like jerky, clumsy beetles. They have men for brains, hunched over in their cabins, along for the ride, parasites. The big digger's windows are tinted the same shiny black as the eyes of spiders Cora asks him to kill. 'Kill it! Kill iiit!' she shrieks. Does she care, he wonders bitterly, that he is a finished man? This is unfair, as she doesn't know. But if she did, would she care?

Thirteen years ago it was they laid the now-corroded pipes, the year the boy was born. Same circus, clunkier machines. Only thirteen years, unbelievable. After thirteen years, everything has to come out. You can count on Irish Water to pick the absolute worst type of pipe, the type that will last you thirteen years instead of sixty. A man can rest easy with sixty. And another thing: you can count on Irish Water to drag out a construction job. On the website, a peppy article forecasts works from May to July, and it's getting to be well into October. If a man has to be finished, let him be finished, make it quick. Don't hammer the nail into his head every God-given morning. Though maybe that's part of the penitence, the waiting. Keeping a man on – what is it? – on tenterhooks.

A courteous honk from behind gets Jimmy to release the brake pedal and to lift one hand in nonchalant apology. The lower he glides on Carraig Liath, the greyer the houses and less flowered the lawns. Ma McDonagh stands in the last courtyard before the two-lane. Her driveway is a concrete square punctuated with dog turds the size of cucumbers. She stands there every morning with crossed arms and stares directly at the drivers in passing cars.

Everyone on Carraig Liath knows her as Ma McDonagh. She lives in that doghouse of a bungalow with her three remaining sons and their women and children, who are often replaced by new women and children. After a while, people started calling her Madonna for a laugh, and then the Madonna of Carraig Liath because she has stood there every morning for thirteen years, rain or shine, rigid as a plaster Maria, putting the fear into every passing sinner.

Hard to say if Ma has taken her cue from her namesake – the singer, not the virgin – when working on her appearance. Her hair is daffodil-blonde with an inch of turf-black root. The frightful landslide of her face is scarred by a red streak of a mouth two-thirds of the way down. Her eyes are raven hatchlings under the fluttering wings of their fake-eyelash parents. Today, as usual, she is wearing a sausage-casing dress under her bathrobe, the pink of which has been faded by time, not fashion. Jimmy catches her in his rearview mirror. She gives up her post for the day and goes back inside. She always leaves right after Jimmy has passed. He wonders if anyone else notices it.

Tom leans on the squad car with the face of a man who has been waiting. They're on Connemara duty today. They have to drive up to Clifden and knock on a few doors to ask questions about a drug network distributing from up there. Recent intelligence points at shipments of cocaine dropping on the Connemara coast direct from somewhere in South America.

Jimmy still thinks of Tom as his new partner, although Padraig has been dead these ten years. Tom is a younger man with all of it still in front of him.

'Alright scan.'

'Alright.'

Tom takes one look at Jimmy's face and gets in behind the wheel. He's often driving these days. They turn out of the Garda parking.

'What kept you?'

'Bit of father-son time.'

They slide into the traffic trudging up the Salthill Road, and the sea starts to unroll to their right. At first, it's grey and opaque, but then a cloud bursts, dumping its bag of gold onto the bay. When they stop at the lights, Jimmy sums up their progress:

'How's the missus?'

'Grand, you know. The same.'

'Ah, you're better off. They'll only break your heart.'

Meanwhile, Cora wraps up in her work-from-home robe, pulls the chair to the desk and her two screens flutter awake. The words on her to-do list, grown cold beside the keyboard, jump at her like dogs, barking in the rhythm of the jackhammer's staccato. She can see the worksite from the window of Katie and Mary's room.

She picked this room for her temporary-then-permanent office for two reasons. Firstly, it gets the morning sun and Cora participates in the Irish sport of keeping the heating off for as long as possible. And secondly, sometimes Cora likes to crouch on her gone girls' beds, to bury her face in their pillows like a goodnight kiss, conjuring up a trace of their smell. The white pillowcases have taken on a rust tone in the middle, where her daughters' foundation stains haven't quite washed out. She makes sure her camera is taped off for that. Imagine if the people at work saw her, the export manager, snouting a pillow with the determination of a fox terrier?

They get regular shards of Katie in the form of Skype calls from Melbourne, where she has taken up with a Donegal lad. Mary, on the other hand, doesn't always pick up when Cora secretly calls. Then Cora worries and can't tell Jimmy about her worry. Jimmy hasn't spoken to Mary, hasn't even uttered her name since the operation. It sometimes feels like Mary is further away than Dublin, like she has crossed some unholy river. It's only the Liffey, though, not the Styx, Cora tells herself. Remnants of her Classics degree always flash up when least expected, asking to be put to work. 'You don't always have to side with him, you know,' Mary had said in her new, toneless voice during their last phone call. 'Women are allowed to have opinions now, *Mam*.'

Her girls were always too pretty, too wild, too bold, too smart, too thick for their own good. And the boy? The boy is a boy. No matter what he does, no matter how bold he gets – boys will be boys.

12

*

'Stop for coffee,' Jimmy grunts when they pass the university and Tom swerves into the parking in front of the Centra. Jimmy struts to the door with two thumbs stuck into his high-vis vest and all the sashay of a cowboy hitting the saloon. Tom never mastered the TV-detective swagger, nor does he wish to. You're conspicuous enough wearing the uniform and driving the blue-and-neon chequered car. A few people eye them, wondering if there's trouble, but most are used to seeing the Garda car pull up around this time. Twenty years Jimmy has been coming here for his free coffee. At first, Tom indulged him in what he saw as a mourning ritual for his dead partner. Then – well, Jimmy always gets his way.

Inside, they wait along a display of purple Cadbury bars that come alive in the October sun. The rays pelt down with desperate end-of-season intensity, a sun that knows it's finished, is going away for a long time. An elderly man in front of them asks for five types of scratch cards, then pulls out a handful of change.

'There's two,' he says. 'Here's another fifty cents, twenty, twenty, ten, that's three.' He turns around: 'Won't be a minute, lads.'

Jimmy's fingers are drumming on the Cadbury display and he looks around as if for something to throw or smash. He's not good at waiting. The jackhammer is in his brain, and he needs coffee to take the edge off. Finally, the old man shuffles off, giving them a nod.

'How's things, Deepak,' says Jimmy.

'Jimmy, how are you this morning? Americano with milk, yes?'

'That's it.'

'And for you?'

'Nothing for me, thanks,' says Tom.

'Ah go on, scan. It's free,' says Jimmy.

'Precisely.'

'He'll have a flat white,' says Jimmy. They move down the counter to where the coffees are made. There's a new girl behind the coffee machine.

'That boy will be the death of me,' says Jimmy in one of his sudden effusions. 'He don't play ball. He don't like cars. God knows what he's up to, half the time. That kid hates me.'

'Flat white,' says the girl, handing Tom the cup. She smiles at Jimmy. It's the misery that does it. The confessing of emotions, especially hurt. They love it, want to bandage it like reverse vampires. And the uniform. The uniform helps. Soft-heart-in-a-hard-shell type of vision.

'I haven't seen you around,' says Jimmy. 'I'd remember you.' The cheesier, the better. Tom huffs. She couldn't be more than twenty-five, Katie's age. Now she shies, blushes.

'I only just started.'

'Why'n't ya give me your number. Just in case of a coffee emergency down at the station.'

Now she disappears behind the coffee machine. Next thing she says is:

'Americano with milk,' and shoves the cup at Jimmy, poppy-red in the face.

'Can't win them all,' Jimmy philosophizes as they head out the door. They get into the car and pull out.

'Your coffee's getting cold,' Jimmy says after a while. Tom doesn't say anything.

'You have to see it this way,' Jimmy says in response to Tom's stubborn silence. 'If some cunt decides to rob his shop, who does he call? He calls us. He's happy to give us the coffee, what's a coffee? No skin off his back. He's thanking us in advance.'

Tom doesn't say anything. They're just out of the city when Jimmy shouts: 'Fuck me!' He holds up his cardboard cup for Tom to see. 'Your one has only gone and put her number on here!'

'Goddamn it, Jimmy,' Tom says, but he can't stop the smile from bursting from his lips. It could be the fact that they're driving out of the city, shooting out of its tight grey streets and into the reds and browns of the Moycullen bog. In the other lane, cars are muddling forward bumper to bumper, but their side is free and clear, a silver band heading directly into the sky. Jimmy slaps the dash, howling, glee emanating from him like heat:

'Still got it! Still got it, boyo!'

He's such a cunt, thinks Tom, such a cunty, crafty, auld divil and yet, it's hard not to like him. Everybody bloody well loves Jimmy.

Not ten minutes past Maam Cross, they come across the accident. Fresh – they're the first ones at the scene. It's in a tight curve so that they almost rear-end the silver Toyota truck. The other car is a square little Fiat that never had a chance. Head-on collision. The Toyota looks virtually undamaged, but the Fiat is scrambled eggs. The spot is scenic, the curve opening to reveal a lake, poured into a hollow of the Maamturks like an extra slice of sky, with an island of pines in the middle. If it wasn't for the destruction, it could be an ad in a glossy magazine.

'Shit.' Jimmy gets Tom to reverse and park across the road, hazards on, while he radios the ambulance. The jack-hammer is pounding heavy in his head. He downs half of Tom's cold flat white, then he runs to the truck while Tom goes to check inside the Fiat. Jimmy has to get up on the running board because of the truck's absurdly heightened suspensions. The man behind the wheel, a block face and low-planted dark hair, turns to him. Well.

'Another fucking McDonagh.'

The man has blood on his forehead – that cunt wasn't even wearing a seatbelt – and the bone of his right arm pokes out whitely. Other than that, a few broken ribs, judging by the way he's hunched over the airbag. He's some relation to Ma. Could even be her brother.

'It's your lucky day, scan.' Jimmy pulls himself out of the car to check on Tom. His partner has gotten in through the Fiat's passenger door and is out of sight. 'First thing is, you're gonna play unconscious. Got it? Can't breathalyse you if you're passed out.'

The man's intelligent eyes stare back at him. He's listening. A litre bottle of vodka sits on the passenger seat like a polite hitchhiker, unmoved by the accident. Jimmy grabs it by the neck, swings, and gets it flying a good hundred feet into the bog.

'Anything else,' Jimmy says. The man blinks, doing some thinking. Then, with a clumsy left arm, he brings out a handful of cocaine zips and rains them down onto the passenger seat.

'Fuck me,' says Jimmy and shoves the baggies into his inside pocket. He looks up, sees Tom backing out of the other car. Then Tom just stands in the ditch, his face grey, arms away from his sides.

'What's the story?' Jimmy shouts.

'Dead. She's dead.'

'Oh, fuck me bloody,' Jimmy mutters.

'And your man?'

'Passed out.'

The deceased is a female in her late twenties. The bonnet of her Fiat was shoved clean through the windshield, and through her neck. Her hand still grips the gearstick, her long nails painted an orangey red, the type of colour that Cora likes.

From the window, Cora watches the worksite get moved up. The previous patch has been blasted open, the pipe swapped out, the wound filled up. Now the machines and the fence are another ten or twenty feet up and it all starts anew, the pounding, the shovelling, the replacing. They must have a map of where the pipe is laid, Cora thinks. A knowledge of the hidden that makes them go straight down at the right spot, like a treasure map for Carraig Liath's water. Strange to think that for thirteen years, the pipes have been progressively disintegrating under her feet, without her ever giving it a thought. Her family drank this water, never noticing that it had become more and more tainted. And now, after thirteen years, everything has to come out. In hindsight, Cora thinks she can trace it. The worsening situation.

Cora breathes in deep and relaxes her features into a smile before dialling the team meeting on Zoom. She has her face on now – make-up on and hair tied back – and has peeled the bathrobe down to her hips. She feels alive with the bracing cold on her arms and chest.

'How's everyone today?' Cora always starts the meeting with a bit of chat. Much needed, she thinks, now that they're so isolated. Her girls materialize in their Zoom squares, mirroring her smile. She seems cursed – or is it blessed? – to be surrounded always by girls and women. Boys and men are few and far between in Cora's life. Just Jimmy and the boy, now that her dad has passed, and those two are slippery as mud, hard to hold. They don't belong to her in the way that her girls and women do. Sometimes – this is terrible – she forgets they exist, full of thoughts and concerns for her daughters, friends, colleagues, mother, sisters, neighbours. Then, briefly, she lives in a world without men.

Cora herds her girls back to the purpose of the meeting. Each in turn, they talk about what they are working on for the day and throw questions at Cora. Cora knows she has to be fully on for those meetings. Sharp, she bats questions out of the park. She needs this credit with her team, this is where she gets the authority to ask them to do things, as far as she's concerned. She's a good manager. Fair, she thinks.

When the meeting is over, she sinks into her chair, closing her eyes. The jackhammer is at her temples along with the nagging items on her to-do list. There are always too many things to do – the work piles up faster than she can get through it. In a way, being a mother has prepared her well for this. It never seems like the end of the chores can be reached, and yet, night comes, the world doesn't end, and another day rolls around. A permanent work-in-progress, like laying a pipe to the moon.

Reluctant because of the cold, she makes herself go on her lunch walk. Once outside, she is glad of her decision. She sets herself a quick pace, marches uphill, away from the pounding worksite. Flocks of migratory birds converge on roofs, giddy as children ready for a school trip. She pushes out some big exhales, feeling that particular delight that comes with seeing the first white breath of the year. She leaves the pavement and goes up past the reservoir, where there is a short path between trees that ends abruptly at the Circular Road. Some things, Cora thinks, can be talked about: the mud-brown colour of trees, the sunless brightness of the sky. Others can never be put into words: the thought that she can smell the rising souls of dead leaves, the sudden, optimistic certainty that all will be well.

'Off for a swim,' Jimmy says by way of a farewell when they are finally back in Salthill. They spent the day with the accident. Tom told the family. They took it hard. Now, Tom lifts a weak hand for a goodbye.

The usual cast of swimmers populates the concrete yellow benches at Blackrock: old men, hard-as-nails mothers, one or two young people here for the jump. Jimmy exchanges a few howayas and takes off his unforgiving boots, the cold floor greeting his soles. He changes into his old red swim shorts, steps up and runs his gaze over the slate of sea, scanning for Padraig's bobbing head. An odd habit he picked up during that week, ten years ago, when they were all out looking for him, and then for his body. In the end, it washed up on Renmore Beach. An accident – nobody would dare say otherwise in Jimmy's presence. It is true that they usually went swimming together, never alone. That day, Padraig hadn't called him.

The biting water grips his legs, then pulls his whole body in, greedy. *I got you bud.* She's in a mood today, sloshing left and right, frothing at the bit. Like waking up or being born, he finds himself firmly back into the present. The rest of the day is now hindsight – future and past no longer exist, only the current breaststroke out into the open. Jimmy lifts one arm to check his Fitbit. He stays in for a full ten minutes, then stays a little longer still, he knows it could be his last swim for a while. He can feel Padraig closer than he has been these ten years. Then he

19

climbs out, the water and fear rushing off him, ready to face home.

Cora powers down her computer and, without losing one instant, puts on her coat and gets into the car. The appointment is at 5.20 p.m. in Moycullen and traffic at this time is always a gamble.

There's been an accident further up, and the cars on the road to Moycullen move along like alligators in thick water. Cora checks her phone, but her text from the morning, asking Jimmy to pick up steaks for dinner, still shows as unread. Jimmy will shove his phone into the bottom of a bag and forget about it for the day. What if she has an emergency? Or if something happens to the boy? She's on her own.

She's late but Dr Felt still takes her. She has been coming to him for over ten years. He ushers her into the calm consultation room, has her lie down on the table. Here, she is allowed to close her eyes in the middle of the day, the bright lamp above making for a red darkness behind her lids.

'How've you been holding up?' Dr Felt asks, leaning in close to her face, marking the injection sites with a white pen.

'Ups and downs ...' She realizes he means the Botox. 'Oh. The frown area has worn off quicker this time.'

'Have you been careful to avoid expressions of displeasure?' Dr Felt asks, measuring out a syringe. She doesn't reply.

The bell rings for the end of the day and the boy jumps up, runs into the skein of young bodies shoving each other at the door while the teacher ineffectively uses his calm voice. The bell is an artificial four-tone song that the boy sometimes hallucinates when a class drags on. When the end of the day arrives, it doesn't just ring once, it keeps going and going, pushing the students into the frenzy of convicts on day release. For years into the future, the boy will hear his old school bell, and it will awaken this urge in the pit of his stomach, this need to run, to get out, to break free.

They're a cluster of lads dropping each other off at the estates they pass along the way. Tommy, who is missing half a leg, swings along on his crutches in the jostling clutch of sweaty limbs. The adults think it's wonderful, simply marvellous, the way they include him. Say they could learn a lot from the young ones.

Now they have spotted a victim, a curbed woman pulling a shopper trolley, coming down the pavement towards them.

'Tommy, Tommy!' Martin howls, red in the face with excitement, and Tommy, the good sport, takes up his position at the outside of the group. Now the lads make an earnest effort to affect polite conversation. When the woman passes, Tommy throws himself at the trolley, crutches clattering, shrieking. They have to admire his dramatics. He adds a little extra touch each time, has become an expert in stumbles.

'Oh my,' the woman says, a hand to her chest.

Now the lads are down, kneeling beside Tommy, solicitous like, *oh God, are you okay man, I don't know, it hurts, it hurts*, until the woman brings out her phone and dials an ambulance, then Tommy jumps up and hobbles nimbly away inside of the loud, wild tornado of kids.

The others fall off one at a time like satiated ticks and the boy is left to climb the dull hill of Carraig Liath by himself. He thinks about how to stay away from the house for the coming hours. He stops at the worksite. The turquoise digger is still at it, picking, scraping, pouring, turning. As usual, one man is operating the machine while three others lean over the pit in silence. Until one of them shouts:

'Wait! There's something in here!'

Jimmy knows as soon as he turns into Carraig Liath. After you've lived in a place for a while, you get to know its moods, its different hours. The neighbours are clustered in driveways, orange with dinnertime dusk, like when they had the power outage. But tonight, everybody has come out, no one is sitting inside lighting candles, the students, the families, the unemployed drunks, the old folks. Jimmy drives slowly and rolls down his window when he recognizes Bea Lavin in a buzzing group. She hurries over, excited at having found a fresh neighbour, unsullied as new snow.

'Jimmy, you're never going to believe this …' He sees her putting the sentences together in her head with that instinct for storytelling. She lingers on the arresting details – the jackhammer stopping for once, the white-and-maroon jersey showing through the rubble, the man dead a long time with his hands zip-tied in his back – and drumrolls up to the final reveal: the man is no other than Darragh McDonagh, the son who disappeared thirteen years ago. Jimmy's fingers, without being asked, remember pulling the zip-tie tight around the man's wrists. That's when Darragh started giving them cheek. Had Jimmy landed the first blow, or Padraig? Strangely, he can't remember. Just that the man had suddenly been on the floor with blood on his chin, spitting and swearing. Then they started kicking.

Jimmy drives on and parks in front of his quiet house. He listens to the car ticking down, the commotion around the worksite behind his back. Then, making a quick decision, he gets out of the car and heads towards the noise. Grapes of people are hanging off the fences. When he gets closer, he sees his boy with his face pressed tight against the metal. The rows of bungalows gape on like they're standing around the dance floor at a teenage disco. Their dumbstruck faces are lit in red and blue strobe. There are five police cars parked at the road and Jimmy picks out the high-vis Gardaí trying to keep his neighbours from running down the fence. He recognizes Lorcan, a new recruit with the eager elasticity of an Irish setter.

'Jimmy, how's things, did you get called out too?'

Lorcan is too young to have been around at the time of the internal inquest, thirteen years ago. Padraig and Jimmy had stood before the ombudsman and sworn that Darragh McDonagh had gotten away from them when they had come to arrest him. There was an anonymous testimony alleging prisoner beatings by the pair, which was considered strong circumstantial evidence. But in the absence of a body, the case had been dismissed. Things had gone back to normal in some ways, but an undercurrent of something remained. Jimmy, the station's golden boy, had not had a promotion in thirteen years. He never made it past sergeant and would never, now, leave the Salthill station to move up to the headquarters in Renmore. And Padraig – well, Paddy had made his own exit, one way or another.

Jimmy pushes his way through the crowd and looks down into the pit where neon yellow mills around a white sheet. Up on the other side, behind the fence, Ma McDonagh looks straight at him. It occurs to him he will have to get used to being separated from her thus, him on the wrong side of the fence. Her sons and their women and children are ranged behind her, oddly still, all their eyes on Jimmy.

Purdy, one of the Renmore sergeants, has caught sight of Jimmy and is charging up towards him, face red as a fresh brick. *He* is old enough to remember the inquest. He grips Jimmy's arm, hard.

'You better get out of here,' he says, not making any effort at congeniality. Jimmy obeys and drifts up towards his cold dark house, leaving the scene, the shouts, the shrieks, Darragh McDonagh's body behind.

Inside, he flushes the cocaine bags down the toilet three at a time. The Clifton Hill water leaps up dutifully, taking away what needs to be taken. In between pauses for the cistern to refill, he thinks about whether to tell Cora. He miraculously managed to hide the inquest from her, thirteen years ago. There hadn't been any publicity. Not good for the force, enough scandals already. She thought he was having one of his affairs – he always had one when she was pregnant. He decides not to tell her. She can have one last night of good sleep before learning that her husband will be spending his retirement in jail.

After he pulls the last flush, he takes out his phone and scrolls along the names. He dials and waits, nine, ten, eleven rings.

'Hello?'

'Hiya, Mary. It's Da.'

The New Irish

2016

Sometimes, in this town, I come across a cardigan tied to a traffic light, or a child's glove slid onto the spike of a fence. A kind person has picked up the lost item and displayed it in this way for its owner to find.

Since moving to this new country, I have developed a wandering skin rash. Every time it is treated, it leaves one part of my body and reappears on a new, surprising one. 'Are you here for work or study?' asks my doctor, who writes my prescriptions for steroid creams.

Evenings, I walk through my new city, mapping it with my feet. If I walk strategically for several hours every day, I might end up knowing its streets as intimately as someone who grew up here. I walk at the time between nightfall and the hour when curtains are shut. Tonight, I see an elderly man and his wife, sitting in identical brown armchairs, facing the window. Their intimacy is too big for talking. He reaches for the glass of water on the table between them.

I go to the pub with my colleagues. I drink cold cider and feel cold in the crumpled dress I haven't worn in a while that smells like wardrobe. My colleagues have golden hair and skin, well-drawn eyes and eyebrows. The circle of their conversation is warm as a nest. I sit on the edge of my chair, silent.

At night, I lie awake and listen to the sounds of angry voices outside, trying to guess which part of my body the rash is going to move to next. I imagine what it would be like to be deaf: a peaceful state, like being underwater.

My colleague Laura has set me up on a blind date with her husband's friend John. 'You'll see, he's lovely, bit quiet, just like you. Doesn't smoke, doesn't drink.' By the time I think of an answer, she is already taking her next phone call: 'Laya Healthcare, how can I help you?' On my desk, the ripped-off piece of paper with John's phone number curls like a startled caterpillar.

The rash has moved to the spot between shoulder blades I can't reach, where it thrives like loneliness itself.

On the phone, my med student friend tells me my deaf-wish might be a form of Body Integrity Identity Disorder, in which a healthy person longs for a disability, usually to become accepted within the community of this disability. She tells me about a man, in love with a one-legged woman, who had one of his own legs amputated. 'I'm not saying this is your situation,' she adds, when I don't say anything for a long time.

After we have coffee, John starts to walk me home but suddenly stops short: 'I left my wallet at Urban Grind,' he says, and runs off. I look after him, suspicious.

That evening, I see a woman with curly brown hair clear cutlery and plates from the drying rack. She takes each fork, spoon and knife out individually, silently, and places them in the correct compartment. Then she picks up each bowl, plate. Her face is closed like a daffodil bud. Another woman with glasses and a fringe comes into the kitchen, and the first woman's face opens like a flower. I walk home.

In bed, I listen to Rammstein with my headphones turned all the way up. When I look at my phone to pause the music, there is a text from John: *Are you free Friday?* There is a persistent ringing in my ear like a printer's error message.

I download the PPS form, copy of my passport, letter from work and bank statement into a neat folder on my USB stick. At the print shop, the man patiently reboots the printer until it reads the documents. 'Are you here for work, or study?' he asks, while we wait for the printer's dry heave to subside.

John lives on the other side of town. When I wake up, he smiles. 'Would you like some coffee?' he says. Walking home in the blinding sun, I imagine being invited for Sunday lunch at his parents' house in Knocknacarra.

When I arrive at my new dentist's, the receptionist hands me a welcome bag containing a mug, a hat, a pen and a notebook, all embossed with the practice's logo. In the waiting room, there's a mini fridge containing drinks.

'Open wide,' the dentist says. She clinks the small round mirror against enamel. 'Are you over here for studying?'

2017
Already a year in Ireland! My aunt has sent me a long email. *Is it becoming your home?* I decide to reply later.

My parents send me five emails a day. *Which flight should we book?* they ask. *How will we find the bus at the airport? How will we get in touch with you?*

I sit on the couch with my shoes on, waiting for John. Under my cold thumb, my iPhone lights up again and again, showing he is another minute late, sometimes two. When I get in the car, he looks up apprehensively. 'I had to bring the bins out,' he says. 'I was showering.' We drive to the restaurant.

At Sheridans Cheesemongers, I breathe in the mixture of cream and damp. *Cornichons fins*, the labels read. *Foie gras entier.*

'I'll have one Sainte-Maure please,' I say. 'And two hundred grams of Roquefort.'

'Are you here for work, or study?' the woman asks, weighing up the cheese.

My parents arrive late on a Thursday night. I meet them at the bus station. They are crumpled and tired from the journey.

'This is Eyre Square,' I say, trying to ignore the groups of people out on the town. 'This is Shop Street. It's kind of the main street.'

'It's so lively, a real student town,' my mother observes with a quiver in her voice.

I lie awake on the couch, straining my ears to hear if my parents, in my room next door, are whispering about the indignity of my living conditions and the mould hemming the ceiling above my bed. Outside, loud voices lacerate the silence, keeping my parents awake. I would kill for a cul-de-sac.

Mornings, we talk of how well or badly the pater has slept. 'I fell asleep around twelve, but then woke up again.' My father's blue eyes, pools of insanity so like my own, dart over the dry croissants I have laid out on the low table. My parents sit on the couch and I sit on the floor. They lean forward awkwardly, pretending to think it's all great fun.

While my father has a nap, my mother and I wander through shops aimlessly. 'I read there's actually hardly any sheep on the Aran Islands,' my mother says in the sweater shop. 'All this is Australian wool.' I try on a woollen cape, picturing myself wearing it when John finally invites me over to his parents' house for Sunday lunch, hopefully soon. I turn to my mother but she is reading her guidebook, brow furrowed. I put the cape back silently.

On Monday, I stay at work late.

'You can go, if you like, Sophie,' Laura says. 'I know your folks are in town.'

'That's all right,' I say, scrolling through emails.

A fine drizzle accompanies us on the way to the restaurant I picked for our night out.

'They weren't lying about the weather!' my father says. 'Always raining. How on earth do you stand it?' Later, they pore over the menu without enthusiasm.

'How long are you visiting for?' the waitress asks cheerfully.

'A week,' I say, tired. My mother's mouth acquires an ironic fold in the corner.

On Wednesday, I linger in Dominic Street, pretending to look at the art shop window. Behind me, the road is being re-tarmacked. The man with the jackhammer wears big yellow ear defenders and pieces of concrete break off like icing under the insistent beat of his machine. I meet my parents and the edges of their questions are pleasantly blurred. 'Is there nowhere to buy insoles in this town?' my father asks, as if from far away. I smile benevolently.

When it isn't raining, I take my parents on evening walks through my favourite streets, but they politely turn their gazes away from lit windows. 'All the houses here are so small,' my father observes.

My mother loves the River Corrib. 'The Carroub is such a fierce river,' she says. 'Like those spring torrents in Provence, remember?'

At the end of their visit, I hustle my parents to the station an hour early, worried they might miss their bus.

'By the way, why on earth did you cut your hair?' my mother asks.

I touch my jagged ends self-consciously. 'They cut it too short,' I mumble.

'You really shouldn't have,' my mother says. 'It doesn't suit you.'

'That's not a very nice thing to say,' I observe, nearing the end of my tether.

'Serves you right for cutting it,' my mother says sternly.

I hug them and leave. 'Make sure these two people get on the bus,' I tell the driver on my way out.

John and I spend three days in bed, happy, ordering Deliveroo. My parents are back home, a safe fifteen hundred kilometres away. 'We should move in together,' I say, without thinking. John doesn't say anything. I picture him taking each piece of cutlery off the drying rack, cautious of loud noises. Gently guiding each to the correct compartment. His hands fastening around each plate, cup, before putting them silently away. How his closed face opens when I open the door.

'Loneliness is as bad for you as smoking fifteen cigarettes a day,' my med student friend says on the phone. I click the lighter on silently.

2020

There is a thin letter from the Department of Justice in the mailbox. I tear it open on the stairs. *Please provide further evidence of reckonable residence* it says in bold, amid other text. I download the payslips from my last four years in Ireland onto my USB stick, into a neat folder entitled: citizenship.

Evenings, I walk, looking into windows, but I am often distracted. Every other car seems to be a black Audi A3, the type John drives. I almost never catch a glimpse of the drivers. For all I know, he might have changed cars by now. Why couldn't he have had an orange Ford?

I call my friend, who is now a doctor, to tell her about a text I received from John.

'What do you think it means?' I ask.

'I don't really believe in getting back together after a breakup,' she says. She sounds tired. 'It just doesn't work. I'm not trying to give you advice or anything.'

After that, I play Dolly Parton on full blast on the stereo, leaning my ear directly against the vibrating drum of my new loudspeakers while looking up support groups for the hard of hearing, although the ENT doctor I saw says I don't belong to this category yet. My eardrum vibrates pleasantly in response, tickles slightly. I am careful to balance it out so that both ears receive the same amount of treatment. The only issue with this method is my neighbours.

'I, Sophie Grandier, solemnly swear true fidelity and loyalty to the Irish State,' I say. Across from me, on the other side of the wide table, the blank faces of the solicitor and his secretary are resting. I carefully watch their mouths to see if they are saying something I can't hear. But when the secretary softly says 'Continue, please', I can hear her perfectly.

Out around Merrion Square, the red brick houses are as unfamiliar as ever, but I am in a celebratory mood, feeling like another brick in their wall. A Mr Whippy ice cream van has pulled up by the side of the road.

'Could I have a 99, please,' I say.

'Course you can,' the ice cream man says, turning the cone expertly. He gives me a smile with it: 'Are you here for work, or study?'

Marmite

It's a dark and stuffy little shop with rails that encourage bumping into other customers. Empty, two-dimensional men hang from the walls: navy blue, black, black and black, here a bold beige or a silver-fox grey. Many of the 3D men who come in are under strict orders to get something black, can't go wrong with black. They are rarely accompanied, unless newly in love, and if that's the case, there's nothing to be done anyways.

From Ella's vantage point at the till there's the cluttered window - backs of dismembered necks wearing ties which claim to be discounted from thirty to twenty pounds, socks, boxes shaped like jewellery cases containing nothing but cufflinks, sure to disappoint a snooping little girl someday – and in reverse, the name of the shop: GORMLESS MENSWEAR. Named after Edward Gormless, father of Martin Gormless, current owner of the shop, and introducer of improvements such as allowing the shop assistant a comfortable seat behind the till, provided she wear high heels.

Much of Ella's day is spent waiting, looking at the blitzes of life she can see through the partial window, faces come and gone in a blink with the occasional unexpected gaze returned. Further away, bald trees with sunlit limbs seem collaged onto clouds that mean business. White-bel-lied birds are scattered like spilt oats on the green. The clouds can switch Turnerian bright in an instant, making Ella angry with their pretence that everything is good and beautiful in the world. Otherwise, she scrolls through her Instagram feed, blitzes of life but less true. Her thumb hovers over the picture of not-even-acquaintances at a local organic coffee shop. She thinks about the Image, how we strove for realism at first (the Renaissance, photography) but have now departed into a generalized aestheticism which she despises, mocks. She decides to squeeze it in somewhere in an essay for her History of Art class – lec-turers are always starved for nuggets of self-thought, no matter how trite.

The door jiggles. Here's one, she thinks, putting her phone down. The door always jams on the first try. Martin Gormless showed her how to unclench the bit at the top in the mornings, but she doesn't do it, likes a warning. She arranges herself Vermeer-like, takes out her book, the half-light from the top of the window suiting her just fine. From her navel up to the deep thumbprint of the clavicle, juices rise. She can remember a time when the job was boring, drawn out; she was a faded rag doll barely saying hello to customers. Then Martin showed her the sales figures from last year. Said she'd get a Christmas bonus if he saw them rise by twenty-five per cent. That was all she needed – a challenge, a competition. It's not even about the money, she says. Last year, it was a German girl, Jana, holding the shop. She showed Ella how to manoeuvre the ancient till, how to navigate the stock room, and how to tell if a suit was too long at the arms or needed taking in. Now, Ella often thinks of Jana's thin, orange hair, her diaphanous presence, her quiet competence, her reassuring kindness, the way she told clients the suit they had picked fitted them perfectly and the gentle manner with which she corrected Ella's mistakes, always taking pains to tell her that she, Jana, had made mistakes too at first.

She's going to destroy that bitch's sales figures. She's going to pulverize her.

The door opens, and she looks up with a perfect face of surprise – the mouth almost comically o-shaped, as if she's been walked in on naked. Her lips are full and soft like apricot skin, and she never wears lipstick or gloss to maintain the illusion that she is unaware of their sensuality. The entrant almost always mirrors her surprise, and then she smiles, and the ice is broken.

This one is a man in his mid-forties, and she quickly gathers a whole basket of information. She has to get in fast, like a surgeon, before the man closes up – which they do as soon as they notice there is a game to be played here. Maybe they expected the acned face of a high school boy or Martin Gormless himself. The man's hair has started turning the colour of a 50p coin but is not thinning; its vitality will be a source of confidence for him. A moderate paunch is just visible under the nondescript winter coat, indicating a wife, confirmed by a wedding ring – bachelors are either toned or have completely let themselves go (she thinks). He has the face of a man who prefers baths to showers. His rimless glasses do not make his eyes appear either bigger or smaller. Enough wrinkles to indicate at least two kids, laughter mostly, the scolding being done by someone else.

A good father, or fathoming himself a good father, perhaps continuing to tickle the little girl even after she says 'no'. His features are washy and classic enough in these parts to make her approach her prey with confidence. She's had dozens like him, in the past few months.

She makes the most of the five steps out from behind the till – has practised them many times, misusing the full-size mirror intended for male and practical use. Her small, hard nipples stand up through her white, tight, slightly transparent shirt. She has taken to wearing unpadded bras to hammock her breasts which are the shape and size of navel oranges. The freshness of her twenty-year-old face is undeniable. By the time she reaches the man, extends her hand, there is usually confusion.

'Let me take your coat,' she offers, having let the confusion tousle the man's greying hair. She gets her accent to shine through and it continues to resonate, reverberate in the man's head so he can't fully focus on what he's doing. She watches patiently, benevolently, as the man uncloaks himself. She has disregarded Martin's instructions with regards to saving on heating expenses and the shop is always warm as a jungle. Doesn't Martin know that heat mellows the mind and body? The man struggles to divest himself, in his confusion has forgotten about the banal scarf – no doubt a present from the wife. Ella can see her clearly in front of her inner eye, as though she knew her, a woman who works some office job of no consequence, with hair bleached blonde, who jokes loudly with colleagues in the sing-song accent they have here. Ella always enjoys this moment immensely, enjoys men taking off their clothes for her, in her shop, while she watches patiently but not without some judgement. She's been on the other side.

The exercise of making a sale, Ella has discovered, is about making a rollercoaster: an up must follow a down, a humiliation must be redeemed by a gesture that will bring swelling in all the wrong places.

When she turns, there's a surprising bum, a shelf that could hold a conversation, unlike the self-effacing ones

worn by thin women in films, an arse as round and big
as the moon that, you can tell, would be jiggled if shaken
– and is, as the heavy coat is heaved onto the hanger – a
departure from the small breasts and hard, slim waist, the
stones of hip points. At that moment, the client usually
notices his surroundings, the sultry French singer susur-
rating through shop speakers a tad too loud – in this too,
Ella has disobeyed Martin who thinks low-volume Classic
FM will give his clients a nice, familiar environment – and
too late, if they weren't really planning on buying anything, that their coat has been taken hostage.

She takes her time with it. When she turns again, the
man has a carnivorous look that jars with his fatherly, com-
fort-loving face. But them's the breaks in sales, she knows,
has been told, or that's what she understood at least. She
fake-mirrors the look with a gracious smile, making him
feel like that's what he looks like too, lip corners curved
up as if receiving a Klimtian neck kiss.

Before he can think of his wife and recite instructions,
she says she knows exactly what he needs, what he needs
is this grey suit that's almost shiny, almost silver. She sees
uncertainty flash before his eyes – she enjoys making them
buy the wrong suits, the ones that are sent by wives, and
seeing them return a week or two later, with their tails soft
now between their legs, murmuring they would like to
buy another suit, black this time. Sometimes they don't
return, but that doesn't concern her, her gambit ends
at Christmas. Of course, they had to tell the wives they
simply loved the grey shiny suit or the electric blue one
that makes them look like a trombone player. Why, otherwise, would they have bought it?

While he changes into the grey suit – *just to try it, just
for me*, for the pleasure of the eyes as they say in Morocco

– she rustles the curtain once or twice when she assesses the man is at his most vulnerable, hunched over a pant leg, paunch at its least appealing dragging down like a full udder, white boyish undies stretched on hairy cracks, high socks on skinny legs. In men, legs turn old first. In women, necks.

When he comes out, flustered, perhaps a little angry, feeling violated by the rustle and the cold shower of the brightly lit mirror in the cubicle – it's time to admire him, there's hope after all. She coos softly and with genuine tenderness. It's important not to appear false now so she makes herself love the skinny arms in the absurd material, brushes down a crease at the back of the jacket like a mother would, takes a step back, gently pulls him in front of the mirror and doesn't let go of his arm there, there they both are, the man in a grey suit and the young woman with the navel-orange breasts gently stroking his arm, and she watches, pleased, as his mirror reflection births a small bird at the crotch that beats like a heart.

After that, when she removes her hand briskly – an eye cast down, the spell is broken, a last plummet – what can they do other than say they'll take it? They hurry back into the cubicle, and if sometimes the braver ones take an unduly long time in there, come out clenching and unclenching a fist, she won't notice, will have been absorbed with something else and be charming at the till. Important to always send the customer off on a good note, Martin said, and for once, she agreed. A good open-ended send-off meant there was space to return for the new tie or correct black suit they would soon need.

It's the hour between dog and wolf when she leaves the shop. Season-wise, it's not quite the dead of winter;

there's a bit of life in the old focker yet. The air is pleasantly laden with decomposing leaves and stars are already getting bogged down in the mud by the canal, which must be carted in from the country in designer bags, she thinks, a feature opted into by the City of London, barely enough to get your shoes dirty. She likes the unfamiliar smell coming out of Boots and Marks & Spencer, the neatly lighted and nestled artefacts, the pavements that always surprise her with their indoor appearance. Ella devours the smell of decay, seeking the paper-cut sharpness of underlying freeze amongst the perfume and chicken wraps. She looks into all the faces, as one would look into brightly lit windows at that time in the evening after lights are turned on, before curtains are pulled. She looks with curiosity, obscenely, hungrily, can't help herself, looking for what? Sometimes a gaze is returned like when she's in the shop, and now her gaze is held, the man walks towards her as if to block the path, a dark figure backlit by the streetlamp. Scared, she comes to a stop.

Tell me Ella, what has become of that sweet young man, the kind boyfriend who was never seen again?

He had become as safe and annoying as a brother; they had become shy of their bodies as siblings would. The way he walked, emphasis on the ball of the foot, was the gait of a younger brother; a semi-colon walk.

'Don't you love me?' he asked.

Ella, alone.

'Don't you recognize me?' the man whose face remains in the shadow says with a wide grin, and then she does, he is one of those she preferred to forget – must forget, the show must go on – for he came in looking like any other, and married his hand said, and left victoriously with a black suit, even came out of the cubicle grinning with that same impudent smile. The discrepancies would have left her unsure had she let them.

She shoos the blood back out of her heart and face. She has wound down for the night, turned it off, and needs to wind up again, but she is tired-hungry. Now she makes herself feel like the man and she are two wildfires that could merge into a headline-worthy inferno.

'How about a drink?' he demands. She hesitates, not sure how to win. 'Cat got your tongue?' he says, what a stupid thing to say, he is a stupid man, and now she has to accept – just long enough to assert her dominance. If she says no now, she'll come across as a timorous little girl, whose 'no' can be easily ignored anyways, he'll never know that she is strong and it is important that he does, or he might laugh at her the way boys at school laughed (kicking her padlock under the locker so she would have to go down on all fours), and she has left that Ella behind bars in the playground.

At Jam & Jelly, it is as though she has fallen into a rabbit hole in her Instagram feed. He apparates falsely light lemony and thymey drinks – them hipsters got some things right, she thinks, eyes lost in the Fata Morgana of golden drink lights, a castle made out of expensive, exquisite bottles – until she hangs in a hammock of spider webs high up, right under the ceiling, attracting looks, huge. There's small comfort in knowing her friends could make fun of this place, its vintage teacups and macramé wall hangings, and of the people with short fringes, cloaked in reclaimed grandmother curtains.

He is talking about art (her subject!), making her feel small:

'You mean you don't know Pierre-Auguste Cot?' Looking genuinely hurt, his gaze gets lost in the lights. He's thinking of more sophisticated, experienced women. The next second he leans in, brushes something (what?) off her face:

'You have the most delicious-looking lips,' he says close, making a trail of nettle stings from her ear down to her shoulder. Breath, sweat, cologne. Want. Don't want. That being said, when was the last time someone had desired her with such class and passion? Dean certainly hadn't, she makes herself think. The man jokes about the suit he is wearing – 'and you wanted to sell me that dreadful brown one' – she cuts him off, petulant like a child:

'I hate your suit.' She blushes with shame; she has let her guard down, shown all her cards, and he laughs, white teeth clinking like cocktail glasses.

'I'll take it off then, will I?'

He peels out of the black, elegant jacket – the most expensive suit in the shop, the one she had sometimes brushed her cheek against, something even her father would wear – and she tries to bring up the judgemental look she uses for undressing customers but it doesn't come. Underneath, his white shirt is taut, starched. She can't help but look at the shoulders as solid as a living-room coffee table, the sloping belly an appealing Sunday morning pillow and – are they his nipples piercing through like snowdrops? It should be ridiculous, but instead all she feels is the unbearable need to take them into her lips, to let him be father and mother at once and more. Her disgusting, chapped lips; she was stupid to think she was pretty before. Who does she think she is?

41

She feels dizzy – is it from the rollercoaster, or from the drinks? She suddenly remembers she hasn't eaten anything since morning.

'Excuse me,' she mumbles and gets up with all the grace of a whale on dry land. She knows her exit is a forfeit, he won't want her now, but she has to get to the bathroom, she feels incredibly nauseated. His playful laugh follows her until she turns the corner. She stumbles closer to the door, just a few more steps, when the fringes of her vision darken. She panics: where is her phone, where is her wallet, she's still wearing her jacket, was the phone in the right or the left pocket?

'I think I'm going to faint,' she says to no one in particular; and next, she's in a dream world, where things are strange but comfortingly blurry, unimportant.

When she comes back to consciousness, it's to a sea of swirling and concerned-looking bearded faces and she instantly knows that the dream world was an infinitely better place. There's something sticky under her hand and her chest is burning cold. The bearded people ask if she's diabetic and if she wants an ambulance, over and over again. She's being fed peanuts and Coke, all on the house.

'No,' she says, 'no, no, no, no, no, no.'

She even forces a smile. She becomes aware of a warm, reassuring presence. Someone is stroking her back, brushing back hair from a sweat-covered face. She has never felt such shame. She wishes they would all just go away. She starts to see the kind person, whom for a second she took to be me: it's a woman with a short fringe and mom jeans. They tell Ella she's lucky the woman was there; she caught Ella before she hit the ground. Ella feels flooded with love. Ashamed and grateful, she takes the woman's hand and squeezes it. Shame, shame, ashamed she is, shamed.

'You're all right,' the woman says and smiles, revealing a gum piercing.

After a while, people disperse.

'Are you here with someone?' the kind woman asks. Ella says she has to go to the loo. On the other side of the glass castle, the man hasn't noticed the commotion.

She drops into the softly lit mirror, surprised at how normal and pretty she still looks. There are the apricot lips and canyon cheekbones under olive eyes, now crossed (some find it endearing). He had taken that from her, momentarily, and she is feebly angry.

It's one of those places where there's only one bathroom. It's on the ground floor and it doesn't look like a bathroom in a bar, rather like your Spanish friend's grandmother's bathroom where you once spewed chorizo stew as a result of too much calimocho. It's got a window that you could easily climb out of – so she does, jiggling the latch (thanks, Martin), remembering to unlock the bathroom door before birthing herself out. She rolls onto the ground in a dramatic stunt-double act and laughs, freed, a child again – a happy flutter comes up in her belly like when she was playing cowboys and Indians. Stealthily, she sneaks up onto the wall, a trellis of ivy grows up it and she climbs, roughing up her clothing but that doesn't matter when you're a child – she drops down on the other side and scrapes her knees, the pain a party-pooper as she now stands up with tears in her eyes. She has become the mannequin behind brightly lit windows that people stare at dully, torn tights and fucked knees.

Car brake lights and traffic signals turn the wet street into a river of fresh blood. She walks upstream until the open mouth of a tube station floods her with white light and relief. She runs down, her Oyster card finds itself after the briefest of panics, she jumps onto a departing train at the platform. She sits with shaking and bleeding legs, a filly after the race, and although she realizes that she has taken the train in the wrong direction – the sudden tele-portation chills her like an icy drink – she has to stay on for another two stops before she can make use of herself again.

At home, she puts on Dean's hoodie and smells it. It wouldn't do to have this scene in a story, to record that she notices how a little bit of his smell drains out each day. She wouldn't be a good character.

But this isn't some story: it's my daughter's life.

My darling Ella. Did your heart bleed, did your soul weep, what did you reap that near-winter eve, far away from home?

Oh, Ella.

Lakehouse Hotel

Once a week, I get to be away from my husband and two little girls.

On Wednesday nights, my two oldest friends and I meet up for movie night. We cook together, drink wine, and gossip through dinner and all through the film, which is usually either in black-and-white or subtitled. Sometimes we go to a nice restaurant instead; our husbands call these nights 'The Culture Club'. Our husbands are good husbands, never complain about having to watch the children on Wednesday nights. My husband usually bids me adieu from deep inside the couch, one excited girl under each armpit like a small gaggle of puppies.

'You go have fun,' he says benevolently, scrolling through Deliveroo's pizza options. I try not to feel guilty for leaving my two precious, healthy babies in the hands of a man whose idea of vegetables includes chips. Beth's husband likes to cook steak on those nights; Beth is a vegetarian. She says she can smell it in the house for days afterwards.

'Sure we all make sacrifices,' Ann says. Ann drops off her son, Caleb, at her mother's house on Wednesdays. Richie left when he was two. Beth and I have long since stopped pitying her, instead silently weighing up the pros and cons of single motherhood.

But that's not all. Every now and then, I tell my friends that Alan can't mind the kids, and that I have to stay home. They throw angry fits, saying that friendship, just like marriage, requires commitment, and to be worked on, and could I not get a babysitter. But they are too tired to hold a grudge. On those nights, I feel especially guilty when closing the door on my sweet family. On those nights, instead of driving to Galway where we usually meet in Ann's flat, I drive to Athlone, where we know no one. I check myself into the Lakehouse Hotel, a few miles out of town, on the shores of Lough Ree. It isn't cheap: the Lakehouse is a four-star hotel with a golf course. I pay using the savings account my father set up for me. My husband doesn't expect me back: I usually spend the night at Ann's, sleeping in Caleb's small bed.

As soon as I step into the muffled, beige lobby of the Lakehouse Hotel, something begins to stir in me. I feel like a little girl, like I could be my daughters' sister. I have to keep myself from giggling when I ask for a room at reception – they always have one available. I don't ask for a specific room; they are all the same anyways. When they hand me the key, I always have a moment of lucidity – what am I doing here? – that quickly passes.

In the ritzy elevator, through corridors, I feel my posture change. I stand up tall, shoulder blades down, walk slowly and with weightiness. At home, I know, my eyes and hands dart left and right like the arms of a crazed machine overheating, one designed to accommodate the needs of two small children. But here, there is nobody watching me; nobody to ask anything of me. On the contrary, I am the person who can ask for things. And I do: I call down to reception for extra soap, order room service and sometimes a cocktail. I divest myself of being a mother – nobody here knows that I am. I even use my maiden name, unnecessarily, when I check in.

And what do I do, alone in my hotel room? Do I let loose, dance to loud music from my youth, drink the minibar dry? No. Do I call a lover? Ha-ha. Why on earth would I do that? No, for most of the five or six hours I spend awake in the room, I simply sit on the corner of the freshly made, clean bed. I stare out of the window into darkness or else at the blank TV. After a couple of hours, I get hungry and call for room service. At first, I sometimes had baths, but I soon found them too eventful. So I just sit there, the room perfectly uncluttered in my peripheral vision, the door perfectly shut, perfect quiet as far as the ear can reach. Safe in the knowledge that nobody will barge in, that there is no household chore I could accomplish, I let the precious minutes of nothingness wash over me. The whole, beautiful evening stretches before me, pale and elongated like the inside of a lamb's leg. When I am tired, I get into the fresh, clean bed without even pulling the firmly tucked blanket out of the sides. I slide myself in and smooth the blanket down. I fall asleep instantly, my insomnia absent on those nights.

On the following mornings, I am often late at work. 'Got stuck in traffic bringing the girls to school,' I say, 'sorry.' Maureen, my manager, smiles and shrugs. She has children of her own, knows what it's like.

Sons & Daughters

There was a breeze of hot fries from the window. The heat outside, uncharacteristic for Lancaster, had earlier tipped into meaninglessness. There was a respite now with the evening clouding in. Keats wiped his sweaty hands on his cargo shorts again and again. He was crumbling weed into one of the strawberry-decorated skins he had received for his birthday a few days earlier. Tom and Curly were mostly silent throughout the process. Others might have become impatient and offered to help, but on this couch Keats was recognized as the best joint roller there was. The way he lovingly included every crumb, keeping a steady pace even at the moment when the roll accelerated and had to be held together for the lick, lent the work something of a craft. Their quiet faces were alternately blued and reddened by ads shining out of the TV.

'Reckon it'll be on now shortly,' said Tom. The sound of his estuary English still made the others, who were Northern lads, look up in alarm sometimes and perhaps this, along with the fact that his hair always looked shiny and flat like a chocolate Labrador's fur, was why no nickname had ever stuck.

'Mum says they're expecting record-breaking audiences,' said Curly, pushing a sweaty corkscrew off his forehead in a gesture that was both childlike and feminine. You couldn't help but go easy on Curly and his runny lemur eyes, even when he said things like that.

Keats – so called because he had allegedly memorized the *Selected Poems* overnight to pass A-levels English, of which he had attended not a single class – licked the strawberry gum. The taste transported him back to his birthday evening the previous week when the lads, ten or eleven of them, had crammed into his room with cans and presents. A rare occurrence: Candace had agreed to attend. He had sat with her at the centre of the bed like a king with his queen, crowded in by Sam on one side and Tom on the other, and had rolled the biggest cross joint of his life. The lads had been sweet, tender almost, handing Candace cans and spliffs she refused, and apologizing throughout the evening for cursing, which she had laughed at. Life was good. Look at the kid out of Morley, straight outta Leeds's armpit, a university student no less, surrounded by higher-education friends and sat next to a gorgeous, sophisticated woman – for she was, a woman that is, a lady even. He had a fierce love for his fancy bird laced with a fear that she could take flight at any moment. Meanwhile, the boys back home were having council flat babies and cheering him on from the sidelines, not even a little bit of spite in them.

'It's on,' said Curly and pushed the volume button on the remote, nestled on the coffee table among an accretion of ashtrays, skins, cables and one of the two remaining plates. All three stayed poised, rendered motionless by the *Sons & Daughters* jingle and Mike Matthews's appearance on set to a storm of applause.

MIKE: Good evening everyone and welcome to *Sons & Daughters*.

He was unable to continue as the normally polite live audience stood in their seats and drummed their feet in a tribal tempo of rising hearts. For a second, the hands and arms of production assistants were seen waving people down until the camera cut to Mike Matthews's face. Mike Matthews was not in the least unsettled, on the contrary, he seemed to soak up the wild, unbridled attention. His signature smile with the top lip rolled up on a row of gravestone-straight teeth never wavered, and his dark, overhung eyes remained firmly locked with the camera.

MIKE: Well, folks, we seem to have a beautiful audience tonight. What say you, audience? YOU ARE STARS! You're ALL stars!

The camera cut back to the bleachers where the audience had risen again and was attempting a Mexican wave.

'Mum says some of them seats went for 300 quid,' said Curly. Keats set the strawberry paper alight and inhaled, holding it in for a while before blowing out a ceremonious smoke ring.

'You'd nearly get a seat at Old Trafford for that,' he said, leaning back with the air of a job well done. Keats's wiry limbs were clad in thin muscles, and a tattoo reading *Carpe Diem* took up most of his forearm. Small chin, small teeth, a skin pockmarked from the acne he had nearly grown out of. One or two spots were still cresting white on his jaw. His baby blue eyes were accented with circumflex eyebrows, giving him a tragic, Shakespearean look girls liked.

'Shocking season,' said Curly, accepting the joint.

'Worst start to a season since possibly, possibly '74,' Tom agreed.

MIKE: Thank you, thank you. We all know why we're here – we're here to reunite a young man with his father. With his father and, possibly – with a million pounds.

Keats had been about to say something but held it back in the general hush that had descended onto the crowd. Mike Matthews was stretching the silence, a contemplative expression on his face. Every breath was bated.

MIKE: The young man needs no introduction. You, me, we have all gotten to know Timothée Dutronc over the past four weeks. We know him and I think I wouldn't be pushing things if I said we have come to love him. These past four weeks, Timothée's revelations have made us gasp, dream and hope, his intuitions have amazed us.

'It pains me to say it, but it's the scousers' year, they couldn't throw it away now,' said Keats, angling it out of the brief pause like a Jenga piece.

MIKE: I know we all want him to win, we all want him to have that million quid, and if I could hand it to him, believe me, I would. But tonight, tonight the future rests on Timothée's twelve-year-old shoulders.

There was *The Flying Dutchman* overture and an abundance of backlit smoke as Mike Matthews stepped aside and Timothée's frail silhouette emerged from backstage. Funny how he always seemed cold, how his oversized, earnest eyes seemed to eat up the rest of his face.

'Somebody get the kid a jumper,' said Curly, coughing up tears and smoke. 'Seriously like, this slays me.'

'You've a bright future in social services, pal,' said Tom, taking the reefer out of Curly's moist and weak palm. It was one thing to go easy on Curly but you couldn't always turn a blind eye.

'We're just a bit of a fallen giant at the moment,' said Keats, continuing his train of thought. 'Let's be honest, the managerial chops are no great shakes. I just can't have one more conversation with any dopey supporters blinded by the legend.'

MIKE: How are you feeling, Tim?

TIMOTHÉE: Good, thanks. Call me Timothée please.

Uncanny how the boy's middle-school English, transported from the Elstree Film Studios, Borehamwood, all the way to the second-grade speakers in a television set in Lancaster, could ring out so pure and true. Like molten glass, thought Keats. Keats's innate ability to sequester such musings made him a rare target when it came to being bantered. The camera was panning over faces in the front row where a couple of strategically placed mothers were already wetting their cheeks, working up an appetite.

'It's a marathon, not a sprint,' said Tom absent-mindedly. With the first inhale, the worry had returned. He had recently started sleeping with his head at the foot of the bed and wondered if anyone had noticed. Then, he exhaled and was okay again. On screen, the familiar montage was playing. The men who had been eliminated were shown performing mundane tasks, fixing their cars or welding together panes of sheet metal. Embarrassingly, one of the men, Robert, was shown shopping at the supermarket, picking up melons and thumbing the soft spot where their anuses would be, a technique he explained was passed down from his mother. Curly wondered if Robert had been angered at that, had maybe even contacted the show to have it taken down.

VOICEOVER: Tonight, Timothée will have to choose one of only two remaining contestants and, if the voice of nature is strong enough, win a million pounds – will it be Jude or Marley? Who is the boy's biological father? Stay tuned to find out.

Two bars of triumphant synth and a swirling ninja star opened back onto the set from top-left view, where doll-sized Mike Matthews and Timothée seemed to be having an amiable muted conversation.

Timothée was moving his lips in the way he had been instructed to while Mike Matthews continued smiling toothfuls of questions at him. He didn't have assistants write them before the show, made an effort to come up with them himself. They were all about Timothée's favourite subjects at school and birthday presents. Timothée was more interested in knowing which of the crouching black cameras was transmitting at the moment, transporting a small, bright version of himself into his mother's living room. He couldn't be sure if Colette was watching but assumed she would be, if only for material.

One of the production guys, Benny, had introduced him to the room where all the screens were being mixed, hoping as grown men do to see his eyes widen in admiration. The cameras under the ceiling were hunched like dangerous but circumspect crows that would only attack after the show, when the lights were off, whereas the ones manoeuvred by cameramen in front of the audience looked like machine guns liable to go off at any second.

If she *was* watching, it would be on her battered laptop, perhaps in the window seat overlooking the Luxembourg Gardens, most likely with a glass of Sancerre in hand. The wine she usually got had corks that always crumbled and he could see her now, fiddling at the corkscrew with the surgical delicacy of someone trying to get a tick out of a limb intact. Her eyes would glide over the park, an oasis of darkness in the desert of Paris city lights. She was the official poetess of the park, she sometimes said, Sancerre swinging wildly in its aquarium. She had published a whole small volume on it, her editor not wrong when he'd said it would sell like *petits pains* in the bookshops up and down the Boulevard St Michel. She was from Paris, *of* Paris, Timothée had always thought dimly. Something of Marie-Antoinette about the red velvet pashminas she sloshed over one shoulder, as if to compensate for the long luscious hair she didn't have, instead a short, black, unmotherly helmet close to the scalp, one curl nestled artistically on the forehead. Her network of shallow wrinkles were the cynical streets of Montmartre and when her mouth opened for a guffaw, most often in response to an intelligent pique, it was as wide and loud and warm as the mouth of a Métro station. Her posture was Haussmannian-straight, but he remembered from being younger – a time when he had sometimes been allowed to cuddle – that the white warmth under her arm was as soft as the morning breath bakeries let out at street level.

She was of Paris, but he himself was of this other city, London, that greeted him out of the Eurostar. He was different in this from her, his own person. He tried to find his own eyes and mouth and stances in the clean, wide streets and buildings of St Pancras, distractedly replying to the network executive who had come to pick him up in the network executive Mercedes. Instead, it was Colette he saw again and again. Was there something of her ingenuine party peals in the bright lights of Piccadilly? He imagined her longer, younger strides, later shortened by the need to accommodate his own, swoosh through these streets unknown to him but familiar to her then, the notion that there had been a whole life before him stirring unpleasantly. Perhaps out of revenge, he decked her out in crinolines, mixing up his tenses as he frequently did when she tried practising both their English at home. He had lived here for the first few months of his embryonic life, and he tried to force his memory back into the womb and beyond, an impossible task. Yet that's exactly what he was here to do. The disagreeable realization that he had once been nothing more than the yolk of an egg had been another surprise, quickly shelved. Colette believed in replying to children's questions with complete honesty and an extensive overview of the topic: there were only a few of the mysteries of reproduction left for Timothée to wonder about.

'Do you miss your mother?' asked the executive, who had soft apricot skin and hair the same colour, as if she had guessed at but misunderstood his thoughts. By age twelve, Timothée had become used to these questions and they didn't throw him anymore. He had deduced early on that people referred to the mother-concept as some version of Colette he didn't know. He had taken to addressing her by her first name shortly after this discovery, when he was around ten, and had been thrilled to find the thinly veiled detail recounted in her subsequent short story. He always read what she published, usually in secret, if only to keep abreast of maternal moods and thoughts. Some of it went right over his head, he pleasantly admitted. He had imagined a son-persona for himself, a pathetic child who always missed his mother – yes, he told the woman, even at school during the day he missed her and she crumpled, cooed and fed him M&Ms the car had been stocked with by a foresightful assistant.

He'd had his fun a while, making it into his mother's stories with childish titbits, planted at first crudely and then with increasing cunning. He had learned what made her tick: wonderment was a prime seller, such as the one he expressed at seeing the fish in the Luxembourg ponds never needing to breathe. A quick light passed in Colette's dull-grey eyes, an addict's joy she swiftly distilled into her notebook while distractedly agreeing to another ice cream. His antics made his mother think he was a bit slow although, as Colette found out with disappointment after getting him tested, not quite disabled. What a book that would have been. She lay awake nights over it.

The station at Brent Cross disgorged a thin trickle of tired passengers, and Timothée sought Colette again. Could she be this pale woman with a hunted look, nearing forty but no closer to achieving recognition? She would have been thirty-nine when she'd had the procedure, Timothée had calculated, she had even said where: the London Women's Clinic, the one on Harley Street. Where had she found the money? The donor had been selected in complete anonymity, his existence reduced to hair colour and special abilities. The executive from *Sons & Daughters* had assured him that they could track a donor down, had done it many times before, just look at any of their nine successful seasons. Most of the men donating were young, between twenty and twenty-five, and Colette would have liked that. Timothée knew by heart her short story 'Choosing Baby' in which a woman (a young woman in the story) goes through the in-vitro procedure, the gynae-cological details of which still made him cringe. He read it late one night, after Colette had gone to sleep, handled the pages as delicately as if it had been the Book of Kells, and replaced it in the correct living room shelf when done. She always slept well after an extra glass of Sancerre. He'd had to carefully sift through truth and fiction, especially focused on the short paragraph where the woman chooses a donor who has dark hair and blue eyes like her, the narrator's, husband. She could easily have changed the attributes. But he had cross-referenced love interests from other stories and found they often had hair the colour of the hour before dawn. Either she really liked the image, or this was a clue. He held the possibilities in a careful soap bubble, wary not to get attached to any. No one had ever won the million pounds, and he was the youngest contestant by far – his predecessors had been people in their thirties and forties. Some executive at the network, perhaps the apricot woman next to him in the car, had taken to his story and sold it as a ratings bonanza. Plus, it was easier to find more recent donors.

The same approach had convinced Colette – reluctant at first, she had finally agreed after a Sancerre-less night spent thinking of her agent. Since the *Choosing Baby* collection from the year after Timothée's birth, there hadn't been any major successes, and even those sales were sluggish. This could give them a boost. Publishing houses were looking for edgy, fresh voices and writing about a game show would be edgy, she supposed. Twelve years ago, they had been hungering for motherhood stories – it was like they wanted you to take a youth elixir and start all over.

Some of the stories from her London time could be reworked, the early days: when she had lived in a council flat that always smelled of curry with Dean, they had poured out of her like inky blood. The stories had not aged too well, but everything she had done since had been false. People thought she was being modest when she said this at ever-rarer conferences. And then the stories had dried up like breast milk when she had walked out on Dean, panicked by the possibility of having too much to write and not enough time for love. She had left nothing but a note. She wrote about his reaction upon finding it again and again, but in reality, he had never called. She had dried out and remained dry until now: she had made her-self fertile again.

'My money's on Jude,' said Curly. 'Look at his hair and eyes. They're the exact colour of the kid's.'

Tom, who was taking Voter Psychology, disagreed vehemently: 'Marley has a tendency to hesitate before answering. So does the kid, before asking his questions. I say it's Marley.'

'How many questions does he have left?' asked Keats, who was reserving his judgement. Before anyone could answer, his phone vibrated under the disembowelled crisp packets that now covered the table.

'Gonna need to make a drop on campus,' he mumbled, typing away. He sent another text to Candace, checking if she was free.

'You're not gonna leave before the end of this, are you?' Disbelief curdled Curly's tone.

Keats's phone vibrated again: Candace.

'Yep,' said Keats, jumping up. 'Business is business. Can't let those Lonsdale bastards keep eating away at my customer base.' The Lonsdale College dealers had more of everything: capital, access to quality products, campus accommodation. Some of them didn't even get high on their own supply. Keats knew better than to compete with them for Lonsdale market share, but lately some of his customers from Grizedale and as far north as Fylde had been defecting to them. Keats had come back from his latest trip home with a new bud, and now it was all about getting it to market. Although he rarely attended any lectures, he sure was learning a lot about politics.

'Leave him – he's been summoned by the missus,' Tom said acridly.

'Whoopa,' said Curly, cracking an imaginary whip.

Keats laughed happily, carelessly. He grabbed a couple of prepared baggies and bounced down the stairs to the song of whipping made by his friends. Outside, evening was floating down its blanket, nothing but a line of light left at the horizon. He would have to be careful on his way to Candace's, he reminded himself. She had campus accommodation in Lonsdale and lately, those bastards had been keeping an eye out for him. A room with its own bathroom, the spacious kitchen shared with only three others. They actually had a cleaning lady. A cleaning lady! He thought it was a joke when he first found out about it. Some resources they had, in Lonsdale College. He would have to shadow walls and climb in through her window. One time the others had tried to beat him up when he was coming out her door and he didn't want her to witness that. His chest filled with pride and joy. He'd get a twenty for each of the bags, and he'd see his fancy bird, he was at university.

It was much later Candace saw his skinny hand knocking at the window and when she opened, he looked up at her with a goofy smile. He rolled himself in and she kissed him there on the floor. The long wait had made her want him. Her laptop, shipwrecked among bedclothes, showed a never-ending garland of YouTube videos commenting on the outcome of that evening's game show.

'I'm on acid,' he said. 'We can't do it.' He had bright eyes and dry skin.

'Well, what do you want to do then?' she asked bad-temperedly. 'I'm tired and I want to sleep. And you're late.'

'That's fine. I'll just lie in bed with you.'

'Aren't you tired? It's three in the morning.'

'No,' he said, and he smiled.

They lay in bed, her trying to sleep and him wide-eyed and intense although he wasn't moving. She was intrigued and disturbed.

'Why can't we have sex?' she finally asked.

'My dick isn't working. Can't do anything on acid.'

'You can't even pee?'

'No,' he said. 'Some guys drink loads and need to pee, and they can't.'

'And then what happens?'

'It's just really painful.'

'Can't it like, explode inside?'

'Let's not talk about this.' They lay there in silence for a while.

'So, we really can't have sex?' Usually, he was the one who always wanted to.

'No,' he said.

'And doesn't that bother you?'

'No.'

'But wouldn't you rather have sex than be on acid?' she asked, slightly offended.

'I don't know,' he said, smiling with parched lips quietly and intensely and shivering next to her.

'What is it like to be on acid? Do you see purple unicorns and stuff?'

'Sometimes, I guess.'

'What is it like right now?'

'Colours,' he said.

'What are they like?'

'Just … I don't know … pink.'

'Pink?'

'Yeah … but they're great.'

'So you just see colours that aren't there?'

61

'I guess.'

She fidgeted. 'You know that *Sons & Daughters* thing? The show?'

'Yeah ...'

'He picked the wrong guy.'

She felt a sadness come on him.

'Didn't win?'

'No. Some of these people say the show is rigged, can't win.' She felt his sadness leak over to her side of the bed. 'But it's okay, don't worry,' she said, and didn't quite know why.

Keats and Candace lay in her single bed, Candace slowly drifting off, Keats alive in pink sadness. Over in Borehamwood, Timothée sat in the dark, silent cameras ogling him, feeling devoured. He had snuck back in after the show. Colette sat in her window seat in Paris, empty wine glass by her side, tapping the page of a notebook with her fountain pen. Looking out into the park, thinking, thinking.

Holding Babies

In my thirties, I began to feel a craving for holding something soft and warm against my belly, against my breast.

I craved the feeling like I craved ice cream on the first day of summer. A cat would do, and I often visited my friend in the country who had a needy calico called Marge. The cat would knead into my arms, turning and turning, looking for warmth, and I could squeeze her quite hard without putting her off. Like any craving, this one was stilled quickly, and after ten minutes or so of holding Marge I started feeling a bit sick, and I started smelling her outdoor smell. She sometimes let out atrocious farts and then I'd throw her off the couch.

It was the same with babies. In cafés, on planes, I contrived to sit next to them. Babies are easy to approach. Just stare at them and, with their total lack of social inhibition, they'll usually stare right back and babble and wave their chubby little arms. I knew that if you look unthreatening and very clean, and tell a mother that their child is beautiful, they'll usually let you hold it. Mostly, I was lying to the mothers and thought the babies ugly. It's not their beauty that makes babies desirable, it's their heft, their warmth and their smell.

After a few minutes of holding the babies, the same nausea would rise up in me. The creature would start exuding facial fluids or else an awful smell would come up from their nappy. I'd quickly hand the child back to the mother, finish my coffee and say brightly: 'Well then, off to life drawing class!' – or something like that. I always made out like I was going somewhere exciting. I enjoyed seeing the downtrodden look on the new mother's face; she would have to deal with the stinky parcel. She would probably have to change it on the bathroom floor or endure some other indignity. Hipster cafés and nice places, in general, are not welcoming to parents lugging around infants and their menagerie of needs. I could see this plainly, and I was a person with no intention to procreate, so why did they seem surprised when it happened to them?

I started out with a bias against children early in life. Look at my mother. She had me and my siblings; a fat lot of good it did her. We had her stuck at home, unable to leave while my father stayed out later and later, until he was reduced to a loud angry voice in the kitchen after bedtime. Later in life, I surrounded myself with friends who thought like me. We traded birth horror stories. Contemporary literature was full of women who told all about the ugly side of childrearing. The older women writers had considered birth and children and marriage to be oh so wonderful, and now the new ones were righting the balance.

There was another thing new female writers warned about: solitude in a couple. They echoed each other in describing how alone one can feel in the company of a man. In fact, one might feel even more alone than as a single person. This made sense to me: it's the tree falling in a forest all over again.

I looked out for signs of loneliness in my own relationship with a reasonable man named Colum. He was gentle as a dove, not as tall as I would've liked, and not at all the sort of man you would picture when thinking of the words 'boyfriend', 'fiancé', or 'husband'. Instead, if you went: 'This is my boyfriend Colum,' you'd see the person opposite nod politely while they thought: *huh! So this one calls himself a boyfriend! Good man! Fair play to him.* Not in a spirit of badness, you understand, more like you'd be impressed by a skinny young boy skipping a grade ahead in school.

There were a few things that had, if not attracted, then at least attached me to Colum. He was different from my twenties boyfriends. The twenties boyfriends pushed their love down my throat and deep into my stomach, and deeper still. Colum's love stopped further up, mid-ribcage, considerate like. The best thing about Colum was that he didn't want children. This was pretty rare. Most of the terrible men I'd come across wanted children, and more than that. They made out like it was a great favour they were doing me, offering me the experience of motherhood. When they found out I didn't want what they were selling, they turned dejected and sometimes rough. They seldom planned any interaction with the kid themselves, other than football in the back garden on Sundays. I couldn't understand it. I was not at all sure these men had thought it through. Colum had thought it through.

I was meeting Colum at the wake. Some third-degree cousin, or was it a cousin of his mother's? I was only there because we were planning on going to the cinema after. Colum had brought a condolence card with both our names on it – he was good that way. We sat with his mother and aunts one room away from the body.

That's when I laid eyes on the chubbiest baby I ever saw. It had white, velvety skin that spilt out of its clothes on all sides like a risen bao dumpling. It was almost inhuman, its features drowned in soft flesh. It looked heavy; I could see the young woman carrying it strain under the weight. Something old awoke inside me.

'Ye are coming to church, aren't you?' Colum's mother said. I was supposed to say that we couldn't, that we had plans unfortunately. Irish mothers don't tend to like French girlfriends anyways, so I didn't mind being the bearer of bad news.

'Of course we're coming,' I said to Colum's mother now. The baby's mother sat down a few chairs away from us, apparently collapsed under the weight of the huge child which she now held half thrown over a shoulder, like a sack of flour, where it was happily dribbling over the back of the chair.

'What about that thing we're going to?' Colum said. 'That's starting soon, isn't it?'

'Oh that,' I said. 'We can do that any time.'

'All the same,' said Colum, half rising in his chair, 'I think we should go.'

I can get a bit nasty when thwarted in my desire to hold a baby. Right now, there was a pull from my navel region and to remain seated was all I could do.

'Family is more important than going to the cinema, *Colum*. I think he would have liked for us to come to mass,' I said.

'I think he would have,' Colum's mother said, stiff with the newness of agreeing with me. Colum sat down. I was wondering how to approach the baby. The best moment would be at the procession. I hoped the wake wouldn't last too much longer. But it felt like for ever before the room finally stirred with the passage of the pallbearers, six men trying to conceal their excitement and to appear solemn.

I saw that there was going to be an additional difficulty with the baby. A man had appeared next to the mother, and the man was Dean, the twenties boyfriend to end all twenties boyfriends. Abominable. She foisted her bulky offspring onto his lap. It was just like him to have fathered such a perfect, heavy baby. What would he do next to annoy me?

We fell into step behind the slow, slow hearse, and I drifted backwards, letting Colum and his mother float away. The baby was just a few feet behind; I could smell it. I know that sounds crazy, but I swear to God, that baby smelled like a bakery, doughy and yeasty and kneadable. Some old man wearing a cloth cap, his face red from a life of drink, started talking to me. He didn't use the murmur appropriate to the situation. The backs of bent heads and necks around us conveyed silent disapproval. It was plain to see that he had chosen me to talk to because I was a blow-in. None of the heads and necks would have engaged in conversation.

'Thirty years I haven't seen the old bugger,' the man said. 'Thirty years, but in death, all is forgiven.' He looked around to make sure people had heard, but the heads and necks affected deafness and introspection. It was clear that he had come with some inkling of a reconciliation. He garbled on, dropping slant hints at what had gone wrong between him and the dead man, who might have been his brother, or like a brother to him. He took some responsibility for the thing that had gone wrong, something about land? Or a cottage in Westport? I wasn't listening. I was getting quite agitated with the nearness of the baby, the difficulty of it.

'And where are you from, then?' asked my new friend. It had become obvious even to him that he was conducting a monologue.

'France,' I said.

'Paris?'

'Yes,' I lied.

'Really!' he said, and 'really!' when I didn't respond. 'Do you know, it's quite rare to meet someone actually from Paris!'

'Really,' I said, though I was well aware of this fallacy.

'Yes, yes,' he said. 'My brother was in Paris once. Oh, I'm not saying he should have gotten nothing, no.' We'd made it to the church and there was some milling about at the door while people tried to file in in the correct order. I managed to slot myself in behind Dean and the woman carrying the baby.

'You know, don't listen to that old fellow,' said Conor something or other, Colum's cousin or young uncle or friend, from behind my shoulder. We were walking down the aisle slowly, contemplatively. I had met him once on a night out and I think we had taken a taxi out to some suburb, Ballybane or Ballybrit, to score a bit of hash, or was it weed?

'It was him that did the mother in,' said Conor.

I was at the end of my tether, internally bleeding with baby envy, so I said rather too loudly: 'Conor, I couldn't give two fucks,' and the holy stones picked up the *ksss* sound greedily and gave it back to me disapprovingly, *ksss*. I hoped the baby's mother hadn't heard. That would be the end of that.

'My name is Joel,' the cousin said, looking injured.

Finally, we were seated. The baby to my left, so close I could have reached out and touched it. The cousin to my right, pointedly not speaking to me. I had decided I would pretend not to know Dean and bet on the likelihood that he would do the same – he'd always had a stick up his arse that one. Someone tapped me on the shoulder. It was that old geezer.

'Let me give you some advice,' he said, leaning forward in his pew. 'I'll tell you this one for free. Have you someone to forgive in your life?'

My entire being was focused on the baby, its smell, its nearness, my plan of attack. Some little-used corner of my mind proffered an image of my mother, my mother in the kitchen, doing the dishes, saying: 'It's more complicated than you think,' in response to my question. I'd asked why she didn't leave my father. 'It's for your own good, the good of you children,' she said. 'You don't know everything I do for you,' she said. 'It's worth putting up with. You'll understand when you're older.'

'Listen,' he said, tapping me on the forehead with a long, dirty nail, 'forgive this person while they're alive. They might have done you wrong, but forgive them. Take it from me. I wish I'd forgiven my brother years ago.' He glanced left and right without moving his head, but the people on either side of him looked towards the altar glassy-eyed, where nothing was happening. I turned around, ogled the baby. It sputtered at me.

'That's a beautiful baby,' I said. I had guessed right – Dean ignored me, continued looking straight ahead, as wooden as the pews. He probably thought this was about him, the self-centred prick.

'Thank you,' the mother said a little stiffly.

'He must be a year old?' I intentionally exaggerated the baby's age.

'Eight months,' she said, and this time she allowed a note of pride to creep into her voice. 'He's a big boy all right.' I cooed with enthusiasm and she gave me a little side smile.

The thing started, the declaring and standing and sitting. I slid my finger through the breath-thin pages of the prayer book. All the time, my heartbeat was accelerating as the moment of the Eucharist drew near. I would make my break then.

We stood again and everyone started shaking hands and doing the 'peace be with you' thing. The old woman in front of me turned around and shook my hand. I could feel the warmth of blood under her dry skin: 'Peace be with you,' she said with genuine feeling. I turned around to the cousin and he said: 'Peace be with you.' Turned around to the old lad and he said: 'Peace be with you,' and he winked at me. Turned to the mother, and she said: 'Peace be with you,' and we looked into each other's eyes real deep, understanding things only women can understand. For these folks, it was just routine, I suppose. But I never go to church, and it softened some hard spot in me.

Then they took out the wafers and everyone shuffled out of their rows, nice and orderly. When the woman next to me stood up, I remained seated and said:

'I'll hold him while you go up, if you like?'

I could see she had made up her mind to carry the heavy baby. Maybe there was some sort of blessing the kid could get at the front, I didn't know. I could see that her back hurt, her arms, her chest. I could see her adding up that I was not a Catholic and discarding this as not an issue when it came to holding her child.

'I'd like to, please,' I said. I had never begged like that before, never had to, I always made it come off as quite natural, like I was the one doing the favour. I wondered if this meant I had reached a new level in my addiction. She looked at me and she saw my need. Dean nudged his – wife? – and whatever he intended, she surrendered the baby to me.

Oh boy, that baby was a fatty all right. Black-clad crotches and bums slid past too close to my face, and I didn't even care. The kid was positively melting into my body, it was so loose and huge and warm. I checked that the mother wasn't looking and I squeezed until it gave a little gasp and spit up on my shirt. God it was heavy. It was the weight of a young calf. I could see my need being filled like the green life bar in a video game. It had all been worth it, the wait, the weird old man, Colum's looming incomprehension.

I started feeling content, and then I started feeling a little sick. As if on command, the baby furrowed its brow and pooped, then looked uncommonly pleased with itself. The sharp smell jumped into my throat and my bile rose to meet it, but I swallowed hard. I could put it down on the pew and pick it up again just before the mother's return. But I didn't want to let go of that specific baby. I breathed through the terrible feeling of sickness and forced myself to smile at it. 'Ga!' it said. Something told me I could endure and even appreciate the awful sides of this baby for another five minutes. The nausea diminished. Now I was just holding a baby, and it was fine, really.

Saturday Night Dinner

Lorelei runs the lipstick over her mouth, dragging half her face with it. Kissing open and closed like a fish out of water, she fumbles for a tissue, but where the tissue box used to be, her hand finds Niall's razor instead. She detaches herself from her mirror reflection with a sigh.

He moved in just a few weeks earlier and his things still lie on the surfaces of her flat like a hair on soup. His bike in the corridor is a misshapen Tetris, the disembowelled gym bag in her neat bathroom the wrong piece of the puzzle. Sometimes, she feels this disjunction when he lies atop her at night. Yet this is what she wanted, or rather the conclusion she came to after years of married friends assuring her, with the faces of those who are safe on the side of inevitabilities, that tenderness and companionship are just as valuable. For a long time she held out, gnawing herself free from one relationship after another as soon as they slid out of passion. After the last one, exhausted, she gave up. The back of his head is still everywhere on the street, glued onto other faces and his car seems to drive away from her, past her, out from under her windows, a dozen times a day. The discovery that love is easy to come by makes its loss no less painful. She simply doesn't have it in her any longer.

She matched with Niall on Bumble and, after just a few months of dating, he moved in.

It surprised them both, the quick ease with which they readily agreed to a life together – that's how little they knew each other, neither guessing at the other's motives. The transactionality of it reminds them both of an arranged marriage, without either one voicing the thought. Once the decision was made, everything fell into place smoothly, as if the rest of the world fitted more neatly around this new arrangement than their previous, separate ones. It's a relief for Lorelei not to have to walk upstream through days at the office any longer, where colleagues used to comment on her womanly strength with covert criticism.

Niall appears in the doorframe, looking suspicious. Not suspicious, she tells herself: the double wrinkle scored between his eyes is what gives him the constantly critical look. This, her married friends say, is exactly the type of superficiality one ought not to get hung up on. She hadn't been there for the many frowns that brought on the double line: had he squinted up at the sun, as a young man working on building sites in Amarillo, Texas, seeking to gauge the amount of time left before the end of the day's work? Or are the frowns for his employees at the pub, which he set up after his return to Ireland? One pours a bad pint, another has let the basement flood, this other one is quitting after just a month to go back to college. The kitchen lads have left a mess again and the FSA inspector is due any day. She listens patiently and attentively, making small observations designed to further his reasoning, only offering suggestions when she is sure that it is what he wants. Behind every great man, her married friends say. So far, the improvements she has induced have not been acknowledged, but she imagines that one day, maybe in a few months' time, he will look back at the incremental changes and marvel at how far he has come thanks to her.

Niall has his own reasons for agreeing to a quick move. You don't run a pub in a town the size of Galway without becoming somewhat notorious. Niall's intentions are genuine, if not romantic. It would take years for Lorelei to get to the bottom of the murky pond of tavern banter. She doesn't normally mingle with the likes of him, she lives in a parallel Galway with European accents. Some of what is said about Niall is true, some isn't. Either way, it's better to get things squared away while she still admires his entrepreneurship, before she starts complaining about the time he spends on his phone, sorting out things for work during their evening film. It could be that she hasn't noticed his varicose veins yet, from the years of standing behind taps – an old woman's affliction, he thinks.

'Where did you say you were going?' Niall asks, sounding suspicious. Not suspicious, she tells herself again. He only seems suspicious because she made up a lie, an unnecessary lie about having dinner plans, when in fact, she has none. Red blotches appear on her chest, they are the outlines of countries without names. She lays an index finger on the warm jugular notch between her clavicles where blood can be felt pumping wildly. She enjoys feeling herself alive like this. She needs time to think – her brain momentarily frozen like a deer in headlights – so she says:

'Where did you put the tissues?' It sounds more accusatory than intended, and she tries to smooth down the edges with a smile. 'We're going to Mona Lisa.' She's pleased. It has a plausible ring to it.

'I'll give you a lift into town, so,' he says, shrugging himself away from the doorframe and disappearing into the dark corridor. The cymbal crescendo of blood floods her ears: awkward as a new foal, the small lie she thought would just dissipate is growing arms and legs.

'That won't be necessary,' she shouts after him. She wanted to send out her voice strong like a Valkyrie but it comes out a faltering paper plane.

'It's no bother,' he shouts back, 'save you the taxi fare.' She leans lightly on the washbasin, interrogating her expressionless face. *Now what have you done?* She's too deep into her own white lie, and not deep enough into her relationship to come clean about it. She was planning on getting dolled up and then, once Niall left, removing the make-up and watching TV in bed. Now there isn't a good reason to refuse his offer.

Outside, the sky is ablaze. She knows because of the orange-lit frosted glass window, a small rectangle above the bathtub, but it's more than that – she can feel it. Sunsets here are like wildfires. They happen suddenly. A sun weak as milk during the day ignites like a struck match and illuminates clouds from below, turning them into God-sized plumes of smoke. The production wouldn't be complete without the smell of burning turf contributed by a thousand small domesticated flames. Like a wildfire, the spectacle draws crowds. Streets are unusually alive on sunset evenings. People wander out of their houses for an evening stroll in the direction of the inferno, summoned by an old, subterranean voice. Niall has heard it too, he has grown restless, she can hear him shuffling up and down the living room. If she draws out her preparations enough, he might just leave without her, she hopes.

She hears a car pull into their loop of the estate. She tracks its progress as it holds its breath for the sharp bend, purrs the engine over the speed bump and whirrs around the corner. There is always a submerged sense of disappointment when she hears a car drive past without so much as a gear change. What is she hoping for? Just a small story within her life that could start with: 'I was in the bathroom when I heard a car pull in. I thought it was strange, I wasn't expecting anyone.' From there, the story could blossom into anything. A character from her cast list of ex-boyfriends might knock on the door, reformed and contrite. Or a Broadway director had seen the reel of the pilot episode she had been in and come personally to offer her a part. Neither ever seem to notice that she has aged fifteen years.

Instead, she has dragged in Niall – as in, 'look what the cat dragged in'. He didn't resist but hadn't exactly been willing, either. The life decisions she makes never seem to happen organically, as they do for friends, and she wonders why. Misfiring brain-to-heart synapses, she fears.

She takes out the Weleda night cream and spreads her mother on her face. Her mother used to kiss her goodnight with skin shiny from this cream. The velvety smell of it is like that distilled essence which can be found curled up under a mother's doughy upper arms.

'How're you getting on?' He is leaning at the door again, trying to appear friendly. She can hear the crackling of the many small fires of impatience that burn inside him and long to rejoin the blaze outside. She wonders what he would say if she spoke of motherly cream, has a feeling that he would want to avoid the topic at all costs. She imagines his childhood in sepia tones, him as a boy dressed in corduroy dungarees and receiving only apples and oranges for Christmas.

'I'm taking ages, I'm sorry – why don't you just go ahead if you like?'

But he only shakes his head. What is this? A blossoming after the fact of a courtship? In a display of gentlemanliness, he seems to say, he would even miss the kick-off for her. She thinks it strange that a publican would want to spend his night off in a pub (not his own). That was how it started: earlier, at lunch, he said he was going to watch the football with the lads, and she looked up with surprise. It could have been a defence mechanism, when he asked: 'And what are your big plans for this Saturday night?', that she replied: 'Dinner with the girls.' Immediately, she wondered at herself – this man lived with her, why was she still trying to impress him with a fake social life? But it had been too late, she felt, to backtrack.

The orange glow is bleeding out of the bathroom window now, and she guesses that the sun is low. Niall's urgency has subsided and he has sat down on the couch, face stripped of its shapes and colours by the blue light of the phone screen. He could have turned on the standing lamp she selected for its warmth, but these comfort-creating gestures, which she cultivated as small offerings of love to herself, are lost on him. She wonders if this will become one of the things that bother her about him. In the beginning, she always collects these small clues of future disappointments like daffodil bulbs, waiting to see if they will grow shoots in spring. That, or maybe the amount of time he spends lost in his phone, convinced that he is doing something utterly important. She reminds herself that she admires this interest in the work. If she had stuck to acting, or found another passion, maybe she herself – but she was never one to see things through.

After shooting the pilot in Dublin, waiting for her career to start, she had beached in this westernmost place known as the 'graveyard of ambition'. She laughed off the handle but as a temporary measure, she applied for customer service work and had been awed and surprised at her new white-collar status. At first, she said: 'I work for a software company at the moment, but really, I'm an actress.' Now she just trudges through monthly check-in meetings where her manager attempts to instil meaning into her repetitive tasks by commenting on specific areas of her performance, trying to make a coherent narrative out of the parade of voices in the telephone.

She thought she would be elsewhere by now. Wasn't that what her teachers at drama school implied when they said that she showed promise? Maybe they were just doing their own jobs. She used to picture herself in a penthouse overlooking Central Park by the time she was thirty. A naive dream against which reality can't reasonably be tallied up, she knows, and yet she feels an ache inside like something is missing.

Niall has taken up his position against the door again. He watches as she applies clouds of foundation with different-sized brushes. Each touch is invisible but, in the end, the effect is that of a photoshopped image in a glossy magazine. She looks at him and smiles, her small pointy teeth white. They remind him of something from childhood, but when he feels the stir, he quickly drowns it in the activated light of his phone. The plumber is coming tomorrow to look at the leak in the pub basement. Someone will have to be there at nine to lock up. Ronan, maybe. He might have the boys stack the kegs during the day rather than having them all close to the ground. Sixteen spoilt kegs the last day. At about a hundred and thirty a keg, that's … write it off. At least all this is invisible to the customer, he thinks. As long as they don't see it, they can continue to imagine the pub as the cheerful, worry-free place they see on the Instagram posts. It's all about the atmosphere, he always says; and not everyone can create an atmosphere. On the bright side, the new chef is coming out with some exciting chow. Soon they'll be competing with the trendy bars and their Doonbeg crab and pork bao. *All the while keeping it close to tradition, we don't want to alienate the loyal crowd,* he thinks, and types up a text to tell Chris, the chef, not to overdo it. *Each dish should have a familiar element. Forget about the jackfruit burger. Maybe at the next iteration of the menu, we'll see how this one goes down.*

'I'm ready,' she says.

The car whirrs, purrs and holds its breath for the curve, and they're off. Night has lowered itself onto town like a lid on a pot, only a thin strip of horizon is still visible out west. The sky has turned into an ashtray. Passing a For Sale sign on a closed bakery, Niall slows the car to a crawl and leans forward to assess the building.

'If you put a pub in there, you'd clean up,' he says, not for the first time.

She is worried that he will linger when they get to Mona Lisa, but he drives right off. Maybe he'd rather not catch her out in her lie. She looks into the bright, warm windows where families and groups of friends jostle for elbow space. She peers into each group, as though her imaginary scenario might have come to life, her friends catch her eye and wave her in. For a moment, she imagines taking her loneliness out to dinner, having it sit opposite her, share a bottle of Pinot Grigio. They make an odd couple, she and her loneliness. A childhood friend she has never managed to shake, no matter how many boyfriends she has attempted to shove in between them.

But she thinks of the looks of strangers and turns away. What now?

Something wells up in her, neither tears nor laughter, but the thought of her roots here. She pictures them like white vermicelli, easily breakable. How did she end up so far away from her ancestors' soil, where the beech tree that gave her family their name has grown solid, wooden roots, reaching down as far as the branches reach up? How many years must she live in this place before she becomes 'from here'? She had thought moving Niall in would finally anchor her, but instead it has made her painfully aware of how separate each person is from another. Here she is, still pretending to be someone else, so he may slot her easily into one of his prefabricated moulds of women. Maybe she had waited too long, had become too used to living alone. She feels a sudden pang of longing for her life before Niall: nothing was a performance, she could indulge in her purest instincts away from others' eyes. Back then, she desperately longed for something just like this.

She sometimes wonders why she didn't just settle for her first boyfriend. He was neither better nor worse than Niall. After a while, she had begun to feel like the suite of boyfriends was a game of musical chairs – now the music had stopped, and she had nowhere to sit. Still standing, she had become too good at reassuring herself: 'You're fabulous, it's not you, it's him.' But men, she had soon noticed, did not like being deprived of the monopoly of paying compliments.

She wanders down the street, looking into the brightly lit bars, wondering how she could join the small tribes sitting around each table. But she takes out her phone, opens the taxi app instead. *Leonard is on his way*, the app says,

and she keeps her eyes glued on the shortening umbili-
cal cord connecting her to the stranger who will drive her
home. She doesn't want to risk locking eyes with any of
the brightly-lit drinkers, for fear that they might recognize her as the wannabe usurper of their evening. Leonard
pulls up. He names the estate where she lives and she
nods, yes. He tries to make conversation but sees that she
is far away, head leaning on the window that is beginning
to spot with light New York rain, and he drives her down
Fifth Avenue, the famous Broadway actress.

Woodlice Lessons

Woodlice and spiders live in the little house on the hill in perfect harmony. At least, they seem to have always lived there, judging by how stricken they look when I move in. I sweep them up and put them out into the high grasses that are their natural home, or so I read in my hypocritical little book on biodiversity. The book extolls the virtues of the woodlouse, very useful for soil health. In the natural world, it's got a better CV than I do.

When I say harmony, I probably mean symbiosis. Woodlice are the ideal food for spiders. They are small crustaceans that have evolved to live on land, and they have shells that spiders can pierce or slide their hungry teeth under to suck out their nutritious little bodies. I like to think they taste like bisque. That would explain why such a diverse population of spiders comes to my house to sample the delicacy.

What strikes me most, when I move in with those unbidden pets, is their utter sense of identity. The woodlice scuttle in a licey way when I unexpectedly open the door. They live in narrow cracks in the frame. When stepped on, they curl up in a way that is supposed to make you think they are dead. To me, it looks like they are shaping their disgusting little bodies into commas to soften me. I can never bring myself to step on them hard enough to kill them. I know, because once I did by accident, and the shell exploded with a little pop. They are totally sure that the crack in the door is where they belong, in spite of my raids with the brush, then lemongrass oil, and finally the insecticide that decimates their population and probably shortens my own life span by several years. They're just going about their business, the business of living, and what am I doing here, in their house? Am I sure that this is where *I* belong?

Same with the spiders. They are proficient at using their long legs to express shock when brushed up or swatted at with a book. Spiders intimidate me with their confidence. One runs along my arm in the middle of the night because it is the shortest route to its destination. When I shake it out of the bedsheets, it lands on the floor in a state of reproach. It's a brown, nondescript medium specimen. The one I find in my coat is in a bad way. It's got yellow stripes on its back, thin legs all atangle. Probably a side casualty of the war on woodlice. What am I thinking, moving the coat where it had set up residency?

Alone in this house, I struggle to define who I am. Sometimes, in the mornings, when I can't sleep, I take my cue from former, deceased flatmates and curl up in the shape of a comma.

The Chicken

Lulu wakes up in a room with its walls ajumble. She can feel it even before she opens her eyes. There's an empty space to her left instead of stone, and the window sounds are for the wrong ear. There's an inner carousel ride while she allows sight in, and her surroundings take a seat. She's not in her childhood bedroom, where she first thought she had awakened. Memory comes back with the unhurried reliability of a Windows PC. She's on the tenth floor of her apartment building on rue Chabaud, thirty years later. Here is the plaster border where, at night, mouldings of flowers dance; here the dark corner where her long-legged insomnias stalk. They're so glad for their new sister.

And here's the urge; it always wakes up a minute after her, letting her believe that it's gone.

Up, there is an appreciation for her own body, for the Greek arch of the foot and the still-flat belly. There is forgiveness for whip-marks of cellulite on aubergine-shaped thighs, a grateful bow for being nimble, a degree of acceptance even for the half-filled water balloons of breasts – they would be no good in a water balloon fight, wouldn't burst open upon hitting the ground.

She tries her best to ignore the urge in her lower abdomen. Her latest defence against her inflamed bladder is to pretend it doesn't exist. It's a tiring campaign and she is losing.

Today, though, today might be different, might mark the end of months of torment, she thinks. She has made herself a weak coffee which she sips with equal amounts of guilt and pleasure. The subdued summer day stretches out in front of her like a neatly tilled field: there will be the manoeuvring out of the underground garage of her building, the drive through Hauteville, into Rennes, where she will be just in time to find a space in the middle of the parking lot. Three years of working for United Pharma has enabled her to fine-tune her morning routine. She will sit in the ticking car for ten breaths before marching into the office like a smiling, wound-up machine. There will be sterile meetings and hours quartered like Laughing Cow cheese, the order of which will wash over her as soon as she sits down at her desk. She is careful to leave the work there. But at the end of the day, five-thirty – she already fears an overspilling meeting – there looms an unusual appointment.

Today, Lulu is going to see a psychic.

She is well aware that this is the bottom of a descending spiral that commenced many months ago. At first, she went to her GP to consult about what appeared to be a never-ending bladder infection. Her doctor prescribed a rigmarole of antibiotics, scans and urologists before letting slip something about psychosomatic disorders. 'Have you been stressed lately?' the doctor asked, ripping paper sheets off the examination table. Lulu nearly laughed out loud. Wasn't everyone? She couldn't remember a time when she could have honestly answered 'no'.

At the fourth visit, the doctor once more offered a prescription. Every time Lulu was prescribed antibiotics, something in her rebelled, and this time, she refused the prescription. Her mother had been against antibiotics and had managed to ward off all her childhood diseases with herbal teas and home remedies. Lulu remembered the doctor's puzzled face, pharma-sponsored biro suspended over the letterhead paper.

'No thanks, no more antibiotics,' Lulu repeated, and the words caught mid-throat. She rose and left, nearly running.

She had a plan. One of her friends had told her about a homoeopathic doctor. 'You'll see, it's like magic,' the friend had said, and quickly corrected herself. 'I mean, science.'

The homoeopathic doctor gave consultations in a room containing a cupboard made of many little drawers, like Lulu's grandmother used to have for spices. The room bathed its visitors in a strong smell of camphor. He listened to the description of her symptoms, let her err and ramble, his fingertips together in a teepee. Eventually, she stopped talking and an uncomfortable silence entered the room.

'I see you bite your nails,' Doctor Eric finally said. She quickly made her nails disappear into fists and blushed. A relic reflex from the days when Mum had been on the watch for nail-biting among the children, it was silly to fear her now.

'I started again after my mother's funeral,' Lulu confessed. It was still odd to be saying it – people usually got a surprised look on their open-air theatre before drawing a more becoming curtain of kind compassion. Because she was in her thirties, it was difficult to imagine her with an old mother. Mothers tended to die of old age. Not hers, she always had to do things differently. She had fallen off the face of Mount Lion while free-soloing with her rock-climbing group. Doctor Eric made a note.

'When did your mother pass away?'

'Oh, a bit over a year ago,' Lulu said vaguely, not wanting to expand on the topic. She wanted to say that it was all right, they hadn't been that close anyway, but she didn't like the have-you-considered-therapy look this usually brought up. She took the herbal drops the man prescribed but hadn't been back, even when the urge hadn't subsided.

It would be hard to pinpoint when exactly she came to believe that her mother's ghost lived inside her bladder. It was a gradual inkling after Doctor Eric and the idea moved into her consciousness somewhere in between reflexology and acupuncture. Reflexology was her friend Elaine's suggestion. Elaine maintained that the woman had cured her bad knee, and indeed she never complained of it on hikes now. Lulu gave it a shot for the same reason that she had everything else – desperation – and as Elaine put it: 'Worst case scenario, you'll get a foot massage out of it.'

Somewhere in that reflexology room, pleasantly thick with warm herbal vapour, the possibility first unshrouded itself. The round, soft-handed woman was explaining in soothing tones that the area in the middle-right of her right foot was linked to the bladder – *yeah, sure,* her rational brain had thought, but without putting up much of a fight – and at the same time it became a seemingly reasonable proposition that, if the bladder can live in the foot, then the mother can live in the bladder. She fell into a doze in this place untainted by ragged nights of missed sleep.

'The skin on your feet is very thick,' the woman remarked from far away, her warm hands touching her with strange intimacy.

When she was young, growing up in the south, she had practised walking on gravel until her soles turned to horn.

It was a pride, she remembered, while a wave rushed over her ears and pulled her under. A day in the life came back, a summer louder than here. She had spied on her mother and her mother's lover in the kitchen. She had stepped on a thistle the bite of which had fed her anger, that day, another summer years ago.

She surrendered the absurd notion of her mother's ghost to the clear evening air an hour later; but it came back time and time again.

She drives into the parking lot reserved for United Pharma employees, finds a spot in the middle of the parking lot, the exact same as the previous days, weeks and months. She parks the car, ten breaths, a smile machine, she walks fast, the tie on her blouse a fledgling kite behind her. Her assistant Carole's haggard eyes are on her as soon as she steps into the white-tiled lobby which always makes her think of a giant pharmacy with all its shelves empty.

'Lulu, hi – how was your weekend – Alessandro cancelled!'

No panic, she tells her inner army, this is what we practised for. The possibility that Alessandro, the guest speaker at the biggest event in European pharmacy, would cancel with a week's notice is among the approximately 100,000 scenarios she has run through her mind during those insomnias. This is the biggest event she has ever organized, and the head of her department has made it clear that not the smallest thing could go wrong. She riffles through inner plan Bs and knows what to do. But first, bathroom. Her days have become rhythmed by the frequent demands made by her bladder. Go often, don't push, do your Kegels, drink a lot, don't drink before bed – all advice from a range of suddenly well-versed friends and acquaintances which she has come to live by, to little effect.

'Get Marchand on the phone, I'll be right there,' says Lulu. Carole hurries off reassured, fooled by her pretend-calm. Has anyone at work noticed her frequent bathroom trips? she wonders, in the sanitized cubicle that has become cloaked in her many fears and worries. The memories of old bathroom trips surround her, ghosts of the times when she sits with her face in her hands, nearly sobbing, and the times when a merry stream lets her imagine that there is nothing wrong. In the calm bathroom, she arranges a Tetris puzzle of phone calls and reprintings, sets aside time for a lightly-toned email to attendees notifying them of the change of speaker. The email begins to write itself in her head: 'Only one week left until the Eleventh Congress of European Pharmacists!' She thinks that Carole's yearly review will have to be moved again – she'll understand – and she will have to ask Maria, from finance, to show the new intern around. Lulu wields her mind like the handle of a well-used spade in which the push of the thumb has made a groove over the course of years. Sometimes, she wishes she could use other tools: she never meant to be an events organizer at a pharmaceutical company for this long, it just happened.

Clunky, incongruous now that she is in the familiar and immutable work environment, the psychic appointment at the end of her workday seems like a tail-wagging dog in a game of ninepins. Should she cancel? The desperate child inside her rocks back and forth dumbly and says: *no*. She needs this – needs *something*.

Youths litter the entrance to the trailer park, cans in hand. Some of them can't be more than fourteen years old. Lulu is conscious of getting her Högl heels dirty in the mud, and more conscious of appearing insulting. Dimly, she is aware of the chaos she left behind at work. She made some excuse and slinked away, so very unlike her. The caravans all look the same and she doesn't know which one belongs to the psychic, her short-sightedness always kicking in at the darndest moments.

'Excuse me.' She stops a woman pushing a wheelbarrow full of fake Converse, painfully aware that she is acting like the woman is a shop assistant. The woman points at the smallest caravan with her chin. When Lulu opens the door, Mafalda (real name Julie) is chopping garlic.

'Ah,' she says, wiping her hands on her sweatpants.

They sit down and Mafalda starts shuffling cards but suddenly stops, freezes.

'I just got an intuition,' she says. 'Do you want to hear it? You're gonna want to hear this.'

'Sure,' Lulu shrugs. She feels oddly at ease, like she's reached rock bottom and brought a lawn chair.

'It's twenty euro extra for intuition,' Mafalda explains, and Lulu pulls out a note as if in a dream, hands it over.

'You've got a ghost living in your body,' Mafalda says. 'In your bladder.'

'It's my mother,' Lulu says, suddenly acknowledging this is what she has been thinking all along. Mafalda stops shuffling the cards.

'I didn't realize we had an exorcism on our hands,' Mafalda says. 'You want her out, do you? It's fifty euro for an exorcism.'

Lulu hands over another note, which causes Mafalda to get up and leave the trailer. She comes back not long after with a cackling chicken under her arm.

'Oh, God! Don't …' Lulu says.

'It's just a body for the spirit to go into,' Mafalda says, and squeezes the recalcitrant chicken into a cat carrier cage. 'There won't be any blood-shedding, not today. Close your eyes now, dear.'

While Mafalda clunks and mutters, Lulu sits so still that her breath becomes a small bird on a balcony whipping its tail. She hears Mafalda coughing up a mouthful of phlegm and spitting it into the ashtray.

'That's done now, dear,' Mafalda says after a short time. Lulu opens her eyes. Nothing seems to have happened. 'It would take a little while now for the ghost to leave the body. I'd give it two, three weeks.'

Of course, Lulu thinks, getting up. She feels cheated. Her abdomen muscles tense, the urge asserts itself. There is a strange emptiness in her, like she has used up a whole pool of options armed only with a spoon. Where does one go from here? Religion? Scientology? She's already down the caravan steps when she turns suddenly:

'Can I have the chicken?' Mafalda suspends a kitchen knife mid-action. She had started chopping carrots.

'The chook?' For the first time, Mafalda seems unsure. 'It's thirty euro for the chook,' she finally decides. 'I'd give it at most three months though, it's skin and bones.' Lulu pulls out more notes and accepts the fluttering cage in return. Is her step lighter on the way back to the car? The youths give her the same bleak gaze in reverse. *What am I doing*, Lulu thinks, pulling out with the cage strapped into the passenger seat. She hopes no one will see her in the elevator. There's a strict no-pet policy in her building.

Lulu grows somewhat attached to Mother, the chicken, and the disturbances it brings. Although it spends most of its time on the balcony, she lets it in at dinnertime and it pecks at the crumbs brushed off the workstation. She lets it sleep indoors. It usually favours the laundry basket. She sometimes finds droppings under a shelf and picks them up with disgust while breathing through her mouth. The chicken's orange-rimmed eyes are perpetually startled and it flees at any brisk movement. If she forgets to let it in by nightfall, it clunks its talons on the window peremptorily. Its jagged walk seems designed to jiggle its jelly comb and wattles. It lays an egg every three or four days, often in the laundry basket. Since the arrival of her unusual pet, Lulu has found the urge receding into the back of her mind more and more as her thoughts have become concerned with taking care of Mother.

Lulu fries Mother's eggs sunny side up on Sundays.

Les Pins Rural Rehabilitation

There's something here to be proud of, I think, tapping the pages of my speech, then catching myself and stopping the tap. I watch London glide by through the taxi window, quaint with all its smells removed and the sepia colouring of the tinted window: the telephone boxes, terraced houses and blue-lit stores selling smartphone covers; the St Pancras Renaissance hotel and a kebab shop combine in the democracy of King's Cross, warped by the speed of the cab accelerating at the green light. Like the car, the driver is sleek, grey, at once unobtrusive and omnipresent.

'And what brings you to London this rainy evening, sir?' He has caught my eye in the rearview mirror and done his duty – his duty being as much about getting his clients from A to B as about providing the proverbial taxi driver chatter. They are outdoing themselves these days, trying to get a leg up on Uber, hoping you will say, once you've arrived: 'I just had the *most* fascinating taxi driver!'

I hear myself answering that I am to speak at the annual World Health Organization event, an engagement the importance of which I had not fully acknowledged until I hear the driver's polite exclamation of deference. This in spite of my superior Gravier's repeated admonishments these past weeks leading up to the event: 'We are making

95

history, Alan,' he said, his voice shaking. 'History! With a capital H!'

I leave the driver's tactful question as to the topic of the conference unanswered, as the tail-end of the sentence I start, 'It's about ...' escapes me and I stare down at my notes, as though I've forgotten my life's work, forgotten the breakthrough novelty of it, forgotten the heart-flutter – quickly tamed – when imagining its consequences on demography and the whole of our society in the years, centuries to come. My work will shape the future, I think.

I focus back on the speech. There's the opening joke. There's the gripping, spirited description of my subject: anxiety. Here, my chest will swell; here, I will leave a space, a silence, for everyone to collect themselves and when I start again it will be in a lower tone, my attitude subdued, all trace of victory and smile wiped from my face as I hesitatingly recount my own personal stake in the project. My wife Alice, I will say, and I will bow my head. I will bow it not out of showmanship, although there will be those who will accuse me of such, my detractors; but because a woman like my wife should never be mentioned without proper deference. Her multifaceted mind and her wonderfully spirited limbs, how she likes to hold up a well-honed thigh at a ninety-degree angle when we are in bed, asking me to pull on it to give her a stretch. Of course, I won't mention this at the WHO – it wouldn't do – but I will let it be clear that there is a perfect entente between my wife and me, and that this is precisely the point I wish to make with a deeply intimate anecdote: the point that anxiety, the treatment of which I have specialized in, is a natural and inevitable consequence of modern life and that this many-headed hydra of anxiety needs to be addressed, and beheaded. This, I hope, will clinch the speech, my audience's attention riveted by the personal tone and the conclusion I have polished and reworded until it ran as clear as the juices of your mum's Sunday roast chicken.

The taxi gently docks in front of the Principal. Before I can undo my seatbelt, the door is opened by a gold-liveried boy wearing an honest-to-God pillbox hat. I step out into London on legs as soft as a fawn's from the journey. The uncluttered air dilates my lungs like a cigarette dilates an ex-smoker's; it seems almost too oxygenated after the heady perfumes of the south of France.

In the lobby, which has the dimensions and general demeanour of an Egyptian pyramid, I blindly walk straight ahead for about a mile until I hit the main desk. There, they give me a card attached to an ingot of a keychain with enough gold in it for a whole new set of teeth. It opens a door on the third floor. Once the boy leaves us alone, the room and I eye each other suspiciously. I sniff: here, as in the rest of the hotel, an expensive-smelling lemony air prevails. I don't mind it so much in the lobby, but I like my rooms to keep their personalities to themselves. I prowl towards the bed cautiously, pulling my suitcase through the deep swell of mohair carpet. The room continues to make assumptions about me: the latest issues of *The Economist, Business Insider* and *Fortune* glare up from the coffee table. They are as disappointed to see me as I them. A hook by the wardrobe appears just where I would like to hang my suit, which I have carried under its protective cover all the way from Marseille airport. When I open the door of the mini-bar, its lack of stained steel makes me imagine the mini-bar-shaped hole in the hotel's last refurbishment budget. After I pour a small vial of Jameson down my parched throat, I let myself fall onto the bed, taking a perverse pleasure in keeping my shoes on over the silken bedspread. The conference is two hours away and I think of my wife Alice, six hundred miles south.

'The malady of modern life is anxiety,' I say to the flood of spectacles and scalps of rigidly parted hair, brightly illuminated. Nobody warns you, I think, about the unexpected number of tops of heads you will see from a stage, an area so little taken care of, rarely seen, the dark side of the moon. 'And as the French say: *aux grands maux, les grands remèdes –*' I pause and harvest the predicted laughter; it is as eager and stilted as I had expected. There will be an undercurrent of rancour towards my having used this simple trick to goad on their vocal sympathy, I know – these people are not stupid – but I have calculated that the baring of my soul later on in the speech will redeem me in their eyes.

'The peril of our time, brought about by anxiety, is what my research team and I have termed "societal exodus" – the massive rise, in recent years, of people leaving their normal, societally-beneficial jobs and roles behind.' Already, I can see the shiny beads of their eyes begin to glaze over as I explain the method and enumerate the details that make the facility at Les Pins so unique, so effective in treating patients affected by a desire to escape from their optimal lives. I had planned on this loss of attention, and here comes my silence. Eyes blink, necks are bowed and raised. Held-in shuffles are completed.

'My wife Alice,' I say, bowing my head. The room is completely silent, tense. You can feel coughs being held in, sphincters being tightened, swallowing reflexes held. 'My own wife checked into Les Pins Rural Rehabilitation facility last week.' I lift my gaze, a humbled man. Their sympathy greets me, floods me. I had expected it, but it knocks the wind out of my lungs all the same. I am Alan Lamberger, and I have devised the cure for anxiety.

Six hundred miles south, a few hours later, Gabriel opens his eyes to the imperfect darkness of his room in Les Pins Rural Rehabilitation. The drunks outside always fall silent as soon as Gabriel wakes up. They discuss the unintended consequences of organic farming in his dreams – is it not enough, he dimly asks, to have researched organic farming for all of one's life, doesn't that entitle one to the types of dreams where drunks discuss, say, the results of the day's races instead?

Now that he is awake in the cottony silence, his surroundings pain him. He is far from the city and its drunks; only trees watch his windows here. He walks to the small window in which smoulderingly romantic pine trees are exquisitely framed, each needle angled just so, still in appearance but with just enough secret movement to send shivers of life through his hungry pupils. And the elegant oak, reaching an arm in the exact direction of God – could it give him a clue to resolve his conundrum with the coat hanger? Although he has arranged the furniture in his room at Les Pins as far as possible in accordance with the golden ratio, it is still jarring. He feels it in his lower back. He has to satisfy himself with this awkward arrangement, where the bedside table spills over ever so slightly into the window frame.

Doctor Francis Rose, the therapist-in-residence, never dismisses his concerns.

Gabriel could open the window and let in the symphony of night air, the note of sweaty pine, the tinkle of the nightingale and the millefeuille layers of earth breathing out in the relative cool. The lukewarm hush would alight gently on his naked arm, more butterfly than breeze. But he knows he can't expose himself to its perfectness; it is wretched enough having to observe the confident pine and God-like oak, and the seemingly random scattering of clouds on which the boldness of moonlight is equal only to its ephemerality. Already, he hears the whirr of chainsaws and imagines the trees cut down, bulldozers turning over the raw sleeping earth to make a flat surface. Cement poured liberally, obstructing the natural airways. He feels it down in his lungs, the familiar shortness of breath.

Doctor Rose suggested his eco-anxiety – as they have together decided to characterize his specific brand of paranoia – has its roots in the tedium of his professional life, where he models scenarios for organic farming in the European Union, a job that is not well paid but for which he is uniquely qualified. The research targets set by his research facility are always missed, and it's his sixth year working on a five-year project seeking to establish what would happen if all European farming was organic. Gabriel is a mathematician, and every day at work reminds him of Zeno's dichotomy paradox: the distance travelled to the goal must first be halved, then the remaining distance must be halved, and so on in ever-smaller increments infinitely. Gabriel often imagines himself still halving minute distances separating him from this one goal as an old man, while around him, the world crumbles. Even past his death, the distance will not have been covered. At thirty-two, he has spent a decade working in various research institutes seeking to promote climate-friendly alternatives – but they feel like ants standing in the way of elephants.

When he had broken down at work, less refined psychiatrists had labelled him a burnout, but Doctor Rose takes nomenclature to be a serious and participative process.

With more sessions, Doctor Rose assures him, it will be possible to compartmentalize the tedium of his work, making him fit to work again. The balance can be achieved by using the vast wastelands of the brain – the famously fallow ninety per cent – as a sort of storage unit. The theory branches off Breuerian hypnotism, where the patient is made to relive traumatic events under hypnosis, thereby supposedly defusing them of their power. This hit-or-miss method would be improved, according to Professor Alan Lamberger, if the traumatic events were simply removed altogether. A result achieved by a deceptively simple combination of speech therapy and mild doses of psychedelic drugs administered under the most comprehensive medical supervision.

This is the revolutionary method developed by Professor Lamberger, whose wife Alice is also a patient at Les Pins. They already call it the Lamberger Method. This discovery is said to be the next step on the ladder of human development, the manifest destiny for those uninhabited shores of human brain space. Understand, said Doctor Rose, that there is no risk of repressing the subconscious – it is widely acknowledged that it has its utility. There is no danger, therefore. He repeats it with confidence.

Ever since he agreed to be part of the trial for the Lamberger Method, there's always a question hovering just above Gabriel's mind, but every time he is about to put a finger on it, it is time for another session with Doctor Rose and the question is dispelled.

The next morning hangs heavy clouds bursting to go over yellow hills. His forefathers tilled this land for three centuries, thinks Robert, the farmer on whose land Les Pins is located, feeding the no-good pot-bellied pigs. He has never seen animals grow so slowly; they got them on advice from the positively glowing woman from the Ministry for Agriculture, who said they were a resistant breed and would be a big hit with their guests. His ancestors lived off the land, he thinks. It was difficult for his father, and difficult for him, but still they raised their sons and daughters on this land; they coaxed, extracted from the land a living in a good and honest way.

And now? Now the farmhouse where his own father was born and died is essentially a loony bin.

'A loony bin!' He shouts it out loud, hurling pumpkin seeds at the Houdan chickens, a ridiculous breed that produces hardly any eggs and whose absurd and impractical feathers remind him of show poodles. The pumpkin seeds are five euro for three hundred grams, and it's the only thing the bloody birds will eat. Five hundred cows, he had; and then, his EU subsidies were cut.

'Damn you, EU!' he screams, stumbling on the assonance, at an overcast sky. Agnes appears in the kitchen door, what she calls her 'lion's wrinkle' apparent. She hasn't interrupted her drying of the blue-rimmed bowl.

'Can you keep it down,' she hisses. 'We're supposed to be an anxiety retreat, remember? We already lost one!'

Oh, she's only too happy. He remembers her now, how she was following the Agriculture woman around with a bright smile, you'd swear she was on *Grand Designs*. Following obediently like a puppy while the woman was telling her how to make their farm palatable to city folks, Agnes taking notes, mind you, actually taking notes in a little notebook he didn't even know she had. Where did that notebook come from? When the EU subsidies were cut, the government had arranged it so they could keep their land, provided they turn it into a facility for the new anxiety treatment. It's no skin off her back, sure. She doesn't have the blood and sweat of her forefathers watering the furrows, he thinks.

'Let me ask you one thing,' he says, entering the kitchen, accidentally kicking over a bucket of potatoes, not picking them up. 'Did you buy that fucking notebook? Did you?'

'Would you let it go already with the notebook!'

Alice walks into the kitchen where an argument has just taken place; it still sits in the middle of the table like a big red-assed monkey. The farmer and his wife are breathing heavily from shouting, but they're quiet now, tense. Everyone! Careful to avoid the monkey's gaze, lest you catch a yellow eye, lest the monster explode in loud laughter, and point a jester's finger at your face. The woman's gestures are clipped, a shorthand version of her normal kitchen movements. The jam is put down with too much force, the lid slides off the butter dish, indenting the soft yellow slab underneath. The man's teeth are clenched in a lockjaw with his newspaper, the quiet seething of his rage has its voice in the rustle of the pages. They watch him work through local news, sports, and the classifieds with apprehension. The weather page is too much for him.

'My forefathers worked this land for three centuries!' He has slammed the newspaper down into the butter dish. The dog leaves the room with her tail between her legs. She's an outside dog, the dog knows; no need to make such a fuss, she was just resting by the stove for a minute. The farmer follows her out.

Entering in their wake, Gabriel takes a seat. There's the shadow of an argument sitting in the middle of the table. He observes Alice, the woman who has stayed, careful to fold his gaze back into his lap when in danger of being caught. This morning, her deflated shoulders and bleached eyes reveal she has a pain; an inflamed organ, he guesses. Since he arrived a week ago, these types of thoughts have been coming to him with uncanny clarity. At first, there were three of them; Gabriel, Alice, and the woman named Chloe. Three pilot patients for the Lamberger Method, all arrived on the same day. But yesterday morning, Chloe left. Their silent gazes followed her as she walked through the kitchen with her bags. Was she brave, or mad? And what did she know that they didn't? She stopped in the door and turned:

'The old gods have awoken!'

At dinner, the TV is on, although Agnes insists on mute for the sake of their anxiety-riddled guests. The conversation appears in large blinding letters at the bottom of the screen. A climate relativist is talking to well-loved TV personality Eva Bauer. The climate scientist is speaking passionately.

Ecologists argue that this climate variation is the most dramatic in the history of the Earth. That is just downright untrue –

'I hope you'll enjoy this,' says Agnes, heaping chilli con carne onto Alice's plate. 'I used the secret ingredient.' She winks expectantly like a game-show host.

'Love?' Alice ventures, the word breaking mid-throat.

'Wine,' says Agnes.

They also argue that the current variation is due to human activities. This is probably partly true, although –

'There's sour cream in the bowl,' Agnes says.

'The food is lovely,' says Gabriel.

But even if it was – so what? Humans are as much a natural consequence of the universe as any old meteorite. Finally –

That's all very well, but what about recent revelations according to which you were a card-holding member of the Nihilist Party from 1989 to 1991?

Eva Bauer has pulled off one of her signature interjections. She has managed to bring a bit of TV-commotion to the farm kitchen and to arrest Robert's forkful of chilli mid-chin. The climate scientist on TV looks unsaddled, his glasses have slipped low on a sweaty nose. He keeps throwing angry-hopeful glances at mid-left field where no one ever looks. Perhaps there is an apologetic production assistant there making a tumble-drier motion with his hands, meaning: the show must go on. The scientist reassures his unseated glasses. In a remarkably skilful waffle – someone must have prepared him, Gabriel thinks – the scientist declares that the climate issue is bigger than political allegiance. Robert's chilli completes its journey. The speaker gets back to his topic.

The success of Eco-centrism in the West is easy enough to understand. Is it not said that society thrives only on great peril or great purpose? The death of God and the end of war in the West –

Alice has her daily session with Doctor Rose. She relives the incident that has landed her here.

That day, she is sitting stiltedly next to Alan at the Bernards' Sunday table. The Bernards are her husband's youngest sister Joanna, and Joanna's husband. Alice's hackles were raised at waves of discomfort coming from the Bernards' youngest child.

'Sure, it's not without its challenges,' the young parents start saying with fugitive miens. 'But it's oh so worth it.' The Bernards' denial translates into them getting methodically at least as hammered as before. 'We still have fun,' they say, eyes like poached plums.

Alice fears the unpredictability of children; disliked it already when she was an abnormally rational child herself. The presence of children makes people more likely to ask when they, Alice and Alan, will have children of their own, a question Alice would prefer not to field. But Alan's sisters know better than to bring up the topic: he has warned them that she will launch into her rant on the undemocratic requirements for propagating the species if they try.

When the child slides off her chair and comes over to her, Alice intensely dislikes the sticky toffee-ness of the three-year-old's hand in her own. She was just about ready to reach for a university-educated red pepper cookie.

'Come,' says the child, not letting go of her hand.

Alice tries to pull away discreetly, but the hand sticks and she worries she will bruise the miniature bones, it would be like scratching someone's Porsche. Her pleading looks are only answered around the table by benevolent nods. The Bernards are glowing with parental pride and Alan's encouraging smile is a fig-leaf to his worry. He knows she's not good with children, as he puts it; which does not even begin to cover it.

The child has led her into the garden and relieved her of her hand, started demonstrating a plastic castle, how its drawbridge comes down – she is wobbly as an upright egg, but focused – the various flag-related features and the plastic sword. The obvious construction shortcuts and cheap plastic colours do not obstruct her view of the glorious kingdom. The embossed *Made in China* writing is empty of geo-economic implications to her eyes. She babbles with a serious joy that is neither intrusive nor show-offey. She doesn't pay much attention to her audience of one. She is happy. Kind.

It's the kindness that floors Alice – it's always the kindness that brings about her breakdowns, in emotional times. She is suddenly weak as a willow and wilts to the lawn, the whole length of her body falling in spite of grass stains, and she starts to cry, in spite of the Bernards, in spite of everything that was ever her, hiccups gaining speed like a downhill bicycle. They're round, lakeside, pebbly sobs. They stream out of eyes and nose and mouth. They're of the red-faced type. The child has stopped playing and considers her with confusion, plastic sword raised slightly in a suspended knighting, physical functions momentarily deactivated for inner world-building. Before it can come to any anointments, Joanna Bernard swoops in efficiently, and the child ascends.

'Really,' Joanna says. She looks at Alice accusingly. Children mustn't see adult tears, Alice suddenly remembers, it isn't done. She is looking up at the mother like she must appear to the child: all chin. Mother and daughter look down on her unmoved. But there's no stopping this bawling and for once, Alice doesn't even try. It's one of the most sensual experiences of her entire life. She continues to perversely relish it while Alan gently hauls her off the lawn and foists her into the car. For most of the cold drive home, the edge of his questions is far away. Her monsoon, her waterfall; her precious bloodletting.

'Bloodletting,' Doctor Rose says now, fingers in a teepee under his chin, attention undivided. He says it without a question mark. The way he leaves long silences in their simulacrum of a conversation often makes Alice nervous, almost always bringing her to tears. She feels them well up as soon as she finds herself in the pleasantly cool room where Doctor Rose holds his sessions. There is always a single tissue, neatly presented on a saucer, for her to use, and Doctor Rose doesn't offer another even when she has soaked it through. To distract herself, she walks her mind, nosing around the trapdoor in the back of her head. The meds put the trapdoor there, she knows: it's like the brain she knows is a house, and behind the trapdoor, there's the rest of the world. She had spent her whole life in this house. She hadn't really believed it when they had explained the process, but it happened exactly like they said – except they could not possibly know what was behind the door. Little by little, Doctor Rose was to teach her to carry her bloodlettings and such to the trapdoor and push them out. They had increased the dosage three times already, the experiment not progressing according to plan. *Subject uncooperative*, Doctor Rose's report would read again at the end of this session.

Behind the trapdoor, there's the power of her untapped brain, compared with which all of humanity's feeble hand movements and philosophies are a grain of dust. The power is that of a thousand Niagara Falls. It's enough, she knows, if she was to let her conscious mind fall through the trapdoor, to keep her busy for the rest of her life. She shudders to think of what she would look like to the outside world: a salivating dummy, unable to perform the simplest gestures. Inside, she would be tossed and thrown on endlessly fascinating waves. She has resisted the trapdoor so far.

Doctor Rose doesn't say anything, seeming to follow the course of her thoughts through the windows of her eyes. She fidgets. Time passes slowly and quickly in turns. Another side effect of the meds: minutes dilate and contract like a beating heart, so that she always has to be fetched for her sessions and meals. This new timelessness makes her feel slightly outside of life. She is suddenly scared of Doctor Rose, the way he sits there with his visibly growing nails and lengthening forehead that begins to tower menacingly over her. His audible breathing is loud in her ear and he begins to give off pink and purple waves, an aubergine alive.

'I think that's enough for today,' says the aubergine, resigned, and Alice slowly gets up and walks backwards to the door, not letting him out of her sight. When she gets out and the door clicks shut, she can hear one of the long nails grow long enough to turn the lock.

After dinner, when the dishes have been cleared, Alice quickly escapes the room where the monkey smell still lingers. The other inmate, Gabriel, always disappears directly after dinner. She decides to go outside into a night that has turned wet, and when she does, she is pleasantly surprised at how welcoming the pecks of rain feel on her face. At the edge of the garden, there are munching ewes with busy pelts, whose satanic eyes follow her pensively. She comes upon Gabriel smoking a damp cigarette. He looks like a schoolboy caught red-handed; then catches himself a second time, realizing it's allowed now that he's an adult. They suspend into the air bits of awkward conversation.

What are you in for

Tokophobia

Eco-anxiety

Those are the cages to which others have limited them. But slowly ghosts emerge, and from the cigarette he smokes, the plumes paint facts and figures; she bums a fag and paints some of her own. Of a kind husband, lovely Alan, who made concessions. Alan's sisters think it would be good for her to have children – say it would settle her. You can believe them when they say: with hungry mouths to feed and silence, you won't be hearing your own thoughts. She often thinks about how what she has would have been called hysteria not long ago.

Her husband has five of them. Five sisters. Twenty nieces and nephews.

Gabriel tells her about his work. He wakes up every morning with a worry stuck in his chest. And all for what? It is mysterious, the profit that derives from his running those strings of predictions. There is a tightly coiled spring in between his temples at the end of each day.

The ewes walk away, dragging with them an unknown blanket that was stopping Gabriel and Alice from saying what they really think.

You should leave your husband.

You should leave your job.

They laugh but quickly stop, each realizing: the joke's on them.

A Life Well Lived

'This one here would go quite nicely with your face,' the surgeon was saying. 'The Olivia Williams one.'

Julia held the iTab away from her, the software overlaying the Olivia Williams wrinkle onto her temporarily smooth skin. She looked distinguished, kind. Shallow, evenly distributed horizontal forehead wrinkles and a few seedlings of elevens – or 'glabellar lines', as the surgeon called them – between her eyebrows. She frowned thoughtfully – now that she could – and her camera reflection frowned with her. When she relaxed her face, the wrinkles resumed their place unaltered. She swiped for the next filter.

'Oh this one, I like this one!' she exclaimed. Abundant laugh wrinkles, a line on the bridge of the nose, and two high parallel elevens gave her a regal appearance.

'Ah, the Meryl Streep.' The surgeon's tone was cautious. 'A lot of our clients like the Meryl, but as I mentioned, I would recommend something that goes with your unique facial attributes. As you have a *lovely* rounded structure, something like the Olivia Williams or even the Hillary Clinton we saw earlier would suit you best.'

Julia puckered her mouth, and her faux-reflection apparated a weave of vertical cheek lines that, admittedly, looked out of place. She swiped again, but she had viewed all the options and was back to No Filter. The first part of the procedure had gone well. Even what she called her 'bitch line', the deep fold at the top of her nose that used to give her a permanently angry expression, had been completely resorbed. All these years, she had borne it like a cross made out of small but ever-accumulating failures: the times when she had forgotten her sunglasses, scolded the children, tried to remember if she had locked the car, or worried about money, or increased her speed when walking past a homeless person, pretending to be absorbed in concerns of her own, or had a cigarette. These things don't make you a bad person, they shouldn't matter, and yet there they were, branded into Julia's face.

Now it was time for the second part of the treatment: the addition of her final, improved, tastefully aged visage. She remained motionless, staring at her temporary face for a long while. The surgeon didn't prompt her; she charged by the hour. Suddenly, Julia seemed to become aware that she was not alone.

'If only we could just look like this, am I right?' she said and the surgeon smiled politely. The room was silent for a few more minutes. Only a hint of the hot city whirred outside. The room smelled disinfectant-clean. Julia had always liked the smell of medical clinics, its sanitary sanity.

'I mean, doesn't it sometimes feel like this dictatorship of the natural …' Julia's voice trailed off. 'Why couldn't I just stay wrinkle-free, is all I'm saying.'

'Of course, that is an option,' the surgeon said in a tone out of which judgement had been removed, well – surgically. She herself was sporting what Julia guessed was a light Alec Baldwin: short, angled elevens, wavy forehead lines. The signature mouth-corner brackets. It wasn't what

Julia would have gone for, but she supposed that, being in the trade, the surgeon wanted something edgy.

Julia pulled herself together. What was she thinking? Of course, she wouldn't be one of those horrid wrinkle-free women. Her friends had warned her that this would happen.

'When you see your baby face, Jules, you'll be all like – bye, I'm outta here,' Sandra had said. Janet had concurred. They had met at Hebe's wine bar, their regular, to show off their new frowns and laughter. 'But stick to it, don't you dare come back a bimbo!'

Andrea hadn't had the procedure, though she was thinking about it too. They all had to admit it suited Sandra *so* well. No one said 'you look ten years younger' – why not just slap a woman in the face? Instead, they all agreed: 'Oh, you have aged *super* gracefully!'

Julia hadn't expected to be quite so taken with her face devoid of all wrinkles. She really *did* look ten, if not twenty years younger, and when you think about it, what's really so wrong with that? For the first time, she empathized with the wrinkle-free women she and her friends made fun of. Her cleaning lady Maria, for one. Maria with her slouchy cardigans, rounded spine and black, visibly dyed, hair with the long, white roots. And then the smooth baby face on top of that. What do these women think, that you can just slap it on and it will fool people? Or were they trying to save on the procedure, which cost a couple of grand, but less without the artificial wrinkles? You can alter your face, but your posture, voice, your whole attitude will give you away. It's jarring. It is simply not done. She wouldn't be able to face her friends, even.

Julia reminded herself that she had always successfully toed the thin line between looking her best and looking fake. At forty, when she'd had her breasts done, she had gone up just one cup to a tasteful C, and she didn't have them brought up to her neck – no, only a 'credible lift', as her then-surgeon had said. Now at fifty was not the time to let go of her lifelong ethos.

'All right. I'll go with the Olivia Williams, please.' Julia reclined in the chair. 'But could you go easy on the elevens?'

Hers was a life well lived, and soon she'd have the lines to prove it.

Cailín

'Sure it was the men started it,' says Granny Olga. Her veiny hands slap a huge body of dough onto the floured table, summoning ghostly clouds.

Outside, an unobtrusive type of rain has started falling, like flickering on a screen. I continue looking out of the kitchen window with glazed eyes, careful not to pull Granny out of her reverie. The adults are tight-lipped about what happened; only Olga sometimes blabbers. My mother says I'm too young to know.

I don't remember much, but I remember Christmases before the Scission. Before my father, along with all the other men, left. I still remember my father's presence: a big, bearded embrace. His large voice. I don't remember his face, but I remember his hands which were as big as shovels. When my father still lived with us, on Christmas Eve, my mother took me for a walk at dusk. We came back to a house lit by dozens and dozens of candles. We opened the door and their merry flames lined the dark corridor, all the way to the living room. Here, a tree had appeared, shining like a beacon. And the best thing of all was the tinkling of a mysterious chime. It seemed to come from everywhere at once. Then, the bell stopped and my father came in, pretending to be as amazed as I was. Much later,

I learned that he used Granny's silver cigarette case, clicking the lid to make the ringing sound. I often think of his unwieldy hands producing this otherworldly music for my enchantment.

At the time, it had somehow mattered, us being Polish in Ireland. I'd heard the adults talking about Poland. Now, not anymore. The only thing that matters is that we are women. Us women are north of St Mary's Road. We have the university, the hospital. The men have town, the quays. Non-binary people have a few streets down by the bus station.

We don't have it too bad, in Galway, they all say. In some cities, after the Scission, the women lost out. Their enclaves are unproductive areas, reliant on food parcels from NGOs. And out in the country, it is said, some women continue living with their husbands. Backwards.

Olga's voice fizzles out when we hear my mother's combat boots on the gravel. Granny looks up, guilty-faced. Her muscular arms rest. She gives me a glance that says: this stays between us. I grin, but turn it off when I see Mumia's face. It's hard, like when she's had to do something she would rather not be doing, like killing the chicken on Sundays. Thin, pale wisps of hair, a clear face with momentarily pinched lips. My mother is beautiful, they say. But they say that about everyone.

I know what it is she's had to do. I shouldn't, but I know. It's Katja. She had her little boy two days ago. Two days is the longest they're allowed to keep one, and Mumia went to the border with her. The men will pick up the orphaned boys and, says Mumia, have a decent go at raising the kids, fair play to them.

'Katenka hasn't stopped crying in two weeks,' says Mumia. 'I'm getting worried.'

Granny Olga shakes her head.

'Wood needs splitting,' she says. Mumia picks up the axe with a sigh and swings it over her shoulder. The back door falls shut and after another minute, we hear the rhythmic clac-clac in the yard, paused each time Mumia picks up a new log.

'Cailín, have you looked after the plants today?' Cailín, that's my name. Not long before I was born, my parents heard the Irish word for 'girl' and liked it. Olga says my father always tried to fit in a little too hard.

I haven't looked after the plants yet. I'm responsible for the garden and the greenhouse on account of my green thumb. It's true that ever since I was a little girl, I have enjoyed gardening. I tend to the heads of cabbage and dig up potatoes out of their long, thin rows like earthy Easter eggs. After the digging comes the planting, the miracle of seeded potatoes, propagating from chopped-off 'eyes'. I used to think the notches in potato skins really were their eyes. I imagined them re-growing bodies and networks of tubers through the back of their heads. And I have always taken pleasure in feeling earthworms under my fingers in the good, moist earth. They are the heralds of a healthy garden. As a child, I used to pick them out of one patch and carry them over to another that wasn't blessed with their presence.

Every day, I crawl along my cabbages and remove every last bit of weed, never leaving any root. I stroke their growing heads. I check behind each leaf like a mother checking if her children have washed behind their ears. The knees on all my jeans are worn to a thin, soft thread. If I find a slug, I nail it to the garden fence, next to its brothers and sisters in various stages of decomposition. Once, we had a mole. It dug its corridors through the roots of my plants and threw up little pyramids all over the garden. I lay in wait at its exit for a whole afternoon. When it showed its soft, blind head, I spiked it up on the old cane my grandfather left, the one with the sharp bit at the end. It writhed for a long time and then died. Mumia said I couldn't crucify it.

My favourite plants used to be in the greenhouse. Mumia built it years ago, when shortages of food affected the divided city. Two rows of salads, a tangled corner of beans, seven tomato plants. There is an enveloping, humid warmth that smells both mineral and yeasty. It feels so fertile I can imagine a seed, held out on my palm, sprouting into an instant magic beanstalk.

Lately, the greenhouse has been making me uncomfortable. But someone has to look after it. I put on my garden boots and drag the soles along the tiles of the corridor. Overnight, the boots have become too small for me, so that I can only squeeze the balls of my feet in. Outside, my mother stops swinging the axe for a moment and gives me a surprised look. She has been giving me these looks recently, sizing me up as if she expected my head to be much lower. My mother's friends say I am shooting up, that although I am only fourteen, I could pass for sixteen. They say I'll be tall like my father.

My mother's arms and face are shiny from the layer of rain that has settled on her. She swings the axe once more, bringing it down so hard that the two halves of the log fly apart. The blade gets stuck in the block.

I kick the chickens away from the door and enter the greenhouse. It was fine all through winter, but since spring, the plants have started behaving downright indecently, especially the green beans and tomato plants. Turning on the hose, I try to remember if they had been like that the other years, but I wasn't paying attention. The tomato plants flaunt their round little ovaries, green and unripe. Some of them are starting to blush into colour, to soften, to sweeten. Inside, I know, they will have seeds, each encased in a tiny slippery envelope. I can't possibly eat that. What will Mumia say when I tell her I can no longer eat tomatoes? The beans elongate their creepy, rugged fingers daily. They stroke my cheek when I pass, startling me. I shrink away, and another set of fingers lays itself on my neck, sliding under my t-shirt. It sends shivers down my spine and all around my belly. And the way all the leaves breathe out at once when the water hits them, languorously, like. I can't stand it.

A bee has made it into the greenhouse. She is intent on rummaging inside one of the tomato flowers, oblivious to everything else. The flower nods up and down passively under her weight, letting itself be taken. The bee flies off, looking dazed, pollen smeared all over her greedy little face. I aim the stream of the hose at her, and she tumbles. I look away. I used to welcome bees into the greenhouse and to let them crawl over my hands and face. I used to love the way their furry legs tickled my mouth.

As soon as I can, I finish off at the greenhouse and drag my too-small boots back to the house. The cabbages will have to do without weeding today. Leaving the boots at the back, I hurry to the kitchen, lace up my normal-sized Converse, and open the front door.

'I'm off to see Shauna,' I shout into the house and slam the door so as not to hear a possible reply.

Shauna is sitting at the old bus shelter, smoking. She has grapefruit-sized breasts that always peek out from her low-cut tops. Though her demeanour and face are boyish, she has long, chestnut hair down to her waist which she takes great care of. My own hair is soft and wispy and never grows past shoulder-length. We start walking up and down University Road, kicking an empty can in front of us for a while. When this gets boring, we stop at the chipper. We look at the brown and beige pictures of spice bags and hot dogs. One picture of an especially unappealing yellow sausage reads: *Battered Sausage.*

'I dare you to go in and say: "I want a big battered sausage",' Shauna says, and giggles.

'Okay,' I say, feeling a pleasurable rise in my stomach. Shauna grabs my sleeve:

'But say it like that: *big bat*ter*ed sau*sage,' she says, spitting out the first syllable of each word saucily. She follows me in. The woman with tired hair behind the counter looks up from her newspaper.

'I want a big battered sausage,' I say, leaning on the counter and leering at her. Shauna emits hyperventilating sounds that signal she is laughing really hard, inside. The woman plops a sausage into bubbling oil and says flatly:

'Four.'

'Four euro?' I say, scrambling to get out my purse. It contains a single crumpled five-euro note from Granny, for giving her a pedicure. Shauna has to sit down on one of the soft plastic chairs to catch her breath.

We walk up and down University Road while I eat my sausage in its cone of just-read newspaper. I am starving and it tastes delicious. I know I'll be ravenous at dinner again. I offer Shauna a bite; she declines with disgust.

'Wanna go down to the river?' she asks.

'No, I have to help my mam with dinner,' I lie, and wipe my greasy hands on my trousers.

'Ooh, mammy's girl,' Shauna jeers as I turn off towards my house. I continue walking in the same direction for a while, even after the road bends left and I am sure Shauna can't see me any more. My heart revs up when I imagine her eyes on me. I disappear behind a tree and look down the road: no one. I turn into a lane to the right. These streets close to the border are mostly uninhabited, and no one is here. Everyone is at home preparing dinner, or having a drink, even the watchwomen. Still, I walk close to the walls and pull my hood over my head. I don't want any old gossip to say to Mumia that her daughter is hanging around the border and isn't she getting to be a real little woman. My mother, a watchwoman herself, is sure to be at home.

I get to the car park. Everything seems to be quiet, as usual. I wait for a few minutes. Then I slink over to the car park's former entrance, which is closed by a huge metal gate. The gate has a bit of give, and it takes all my strength to move it by an inch. Then, there's a space big enough for a thin fourteen-year-old to pull through. The concrete wall rasps against my jeans. If my ass gets any bigger, I won't be able to fit anymore. I cross the abandoned, silent car park. On the other side, there's a similar gate, but with much thicker bars and not even a sliver of space on the side. I can see the men's side, the Harbour Hotel and the half-finished glass-and-metal office building. I press my simmering face to the metal. It looks like Colin isn't here. I push down the wave of disappointment welling up in my throat.

'Hey,' he says, breathing right into my ear. I am floored by a surge of desire. We spend a while with our faces pressed against the bars, breathing into each other. At night, when I miss him, it's the smell of his breath I want. His clothes are always damp and salty from the sea. Like many Galway men, Colin is going to be a fisherman.

After the Scission, men started fishing and women started farming. On our side, the land side, gardens sprang up on every patch of bare earth, in the city, in gardens, on rooftops. For a few years, we women ate vegetables and what meat we could produce, until trade and industry resumed. Men – Colin tells me – eat fish and seaweed at every meal.

'Did you find out anything?' I ask. We pretend to be meeting only to share information on what happened before the Scission.

'Not really,' he says, looking at my mouth. 'You?'

'My granny says it was the men who started it,' I say, to say something.

'Ah. And did you find out anything from your mum?'

'Not really,' I say, uncomfortable at the thought of Mumia.

'Ah,' he says, pushing his fingers through the bars to lay them on my cheek. If his hands get any bigger, he will no longer be able to do this, and then what? A cold shower runs from my face to my neck and down the centre of my body. I tell him about the battered sausage and we laugh. I ask him if they have sausages there. He says they do, but that they are round like doughnuts. Things are not very different on the men's side, from what I gather. I turn my face like a sunflower so that his fingers rest on my lips, light as a bee. His cheeks are red and his own mouth is half-open. He pushes his index finger in and I open my mouth like an obedient little girl. Greedily, I take in his whole finger. I close my eyes to taste him better. Would a bean on the vine taste like this? Or an unripe tomato? When I let his finger slide out of my mouth, it smells like my greenhouse. Yeasty from my saliva, and mineral with whatever he has been doing today.

'I have to go,' I say, and turn away.

'Cailín,' he says, but I don't stop walking. 'See you tomorrow,' he shouts, but I pretend I don't hear him.

The next day after school, my steps lead me to Katja's door. Katja is my mother's best friend, and my godmother. When I was younger, she often knelt down to my level and whispered in my ear. She explained that if I had an issue I didn't want to talk to Mumia about, I could come to her. It seemed important that I should know this.

The door to Katja's flat is ajar, as if it was the entrance to a dead person's house. Inside, I am greeted by an unusual sly smell of sour milk and stale bread. The curtains look like they haven't been opened all day. When I see Katja's shape, swaddled in blankets on the couch, I think at first that she really is dead. But then, stepping closer, I catch the glint of her half-opened eyes. Katja usually greets me as if I was a long-awaited miracle, but today, she doesn't move. Only her eyes move.

'My mum doesn't know I'm here,' I say, to say something. Mumia said I was not to visit Katja, that she was sick and couldn't deal with me right now. I almost regret not listening to her. Almost, but not quite. Today, Katja isn't enveloping me in her cheerfulness, but still I am drawn to this mass of flesh and bones that was once her. It's like the time Shauna and I found a dead dog by the river and poked it with a stick, then cut its belly open. All the intestines spilled out and the smell jumped into our throats. I wonder if all of Katja's intestines have spilt out and if that is why she holds herself together with all those blankets. I wish I could ask to see her downstairs mess.

Instead, I look at her eyes. They are paler than usual, like a cup of tea with too much milk. No longer the entrance to a person called Katja, there is nothing behind the eyes today. Or else, everything: a universe. Katja must be floating somewhere in this galaxy, but she is like a grain of sand lost in the Milky Way. A grain of sand, or even a person, would be so small in there that they would be almost theoretical. The hope of finding them would be so close to zero, it's not even worth mentioning. A hopeless endeavour. Katja's eyes remind me of the eyes of potatoes that have had the rest of their bodies cut off. I imagine her regrowing networks of tubers through the back of her head in spring, and my stomach lurches. I look at Katja's hand resting on the blanket: it is like a glove that still has the shape of the hand just slid out. The same goes for her arms, her face. Her hair is like a bad theatre wig. Imagine a person with all its body parts intact, but the thing that made it a person slipped out.

'What you ştaring at.'

Katja's words are slurred, as though her tongue and cheeks were swollen. In fact, her whole face is swollen, not unlike the dead dog. The skin on her lips is shiny from being stretched, her eyes are puffy. Her whole body is risen like fresh dough. It looks as if someone had pummelled every inch of her, being careful not to leave any marks. When I don't say anything, she adds:

'You see, I've been destroyed by two men: one that entered me, and one that came out of me.' Bubbles of yellow saliva appear at her mouth corners.

At first, I think I misheard. No one speaks like this here. They may have done in the past. But now, every woman who gets pregnant maintains it was through IVF from Donor Zero. Donor Zero is what they call the frozen vials that are stored in the hospital. If a woman wishes to have children, she gets herself inseminated with a girl embryo. It is common knowledge, though, that not all pregnancies are from Donor Zero. There are up to ten per cent more pregnancies than successful inseminations, according to a headline I once saw in the paper. And some women choose to give birth to their male babies, even though they know they won't keep them. I know all this. What does Mumia think, I can't read the paper? Everyone knows. It's just that no one says it. No one that's right in the head, anyways.

I sidle up closer to Katja until I am at the exact distance there would be between a priestess and her confessant. She opens her mouth again:

'Men are like cats: they can't be trained. Turn your back and they're up on the kitchen counter.'

She closes her eyes and seems to fall asleep. I wait for another five minutes and leave. Unasked questions follow me out the door.

On Sunday, Mumia sends me out to buy flour before lunch. The streets are quiet: everyone is at home, preparing Sunday roast or drinking. On the way back from the shop, I catch a glimpse of a figure turning into the street that leads to the border. She wears her hood down low, but I recognize her long, brown hair. In the morning sun, it shines like the coat of a healthy filly.

A drumming in my throat: I stop. Something prevents me from calling Shauna's name. I follow at a distance, clutching the bag of flour to my belly like an emotional support pet. At the car park, the gate is pushed open by an inch, wide enough for a young woman with grapefruit-sized breasts. I wrench myself through, pulling a long sliver of skin off my lower back. Warm blood starts melting into my pants, but the pain is as dull as a faraway shout.

Shauna's eyes are closed, her back is pressed to the metal gate. On the other side, Colin's face is buried in handfuls and handfuls of hair. 'Shauna,' he says into her ear. 'Shauna, Shauna, Shauna.' I can see she is sweating with desire. Her eyes snap open.

'Cailín!' she shouts.

I turn and run. Hitting my head on the gate, scraping concrete into my bloody back, I stumble out, run and run. The streets zoom past as if in a video game.

When I come into the kitchen, Mumia and Granny look at me, suddenly silent.

'Did you see a ghost?' Granny Olga says.

'Have you killed the chicken yet?' I ask. 'I'm ready to kill my first chicken, Mumia.'

My mother opens her mouth to say something, but then shrugs and leads me out to the garden. The chicken hangs upside-down above a bucket, its feet tied to the washing line. It's a young cockerel that has already started picking fights with Coco, our rooster, and going after the hens. All the blood gone to its head; it hangs quite still. I encircle its neck, squishing the small wattles, and it starts squirming. Mumia, tight-lipped, hands me the curved knife. I pull down and cut through, swift, like I've seen her do. There is bone under the blade and I continue cutting, heedless of the chicken's now wild thrashing. A leg comes loose from its bind and the claw jitters against the sky, like it's running away upside-down. I cut and cut until the knife comes out on the other side. I drop the head into the bucket. The body is swinging to and fro violently, moved by the running legs. The blood starts gushing out of the neck and paints me from top to bottom. The warm streak runs down my face. I lick it off my lips and it tastes mineral and doughy both at once. Still, my rage gets hungrier and hungrier. I wipe the

126

blood into my mouth. It is not enough. I stamp my foot on a cabbage over and over again until it is ground into the earth. I storm into the greenhouse, where the peaceful smell pushes my anger into a white blindness. I pull handfuls of green-bean-fingers off stalks. I squash unripe tomatoes into a mush and sling them at the plastic walls. Spotting a bee stuck in a tomato flower, I tear off the flower and squeeze it, bee and all, until the buzzing stops. A paralysing sting hits my palm. The pain releases me and I fall to the floor and sob, stuffing my mouth with handfuls of earth.

Later, Mumia comes to the greenhouse.

'Come on, Cailín. I've drawn you a bath.'

She takes me by the hand and I follow her like an obedient little girl. She peels off all my clothes and leads me into the hot water. She washes the blood, earth and pulp off my body, humming an old lullaby. When she has cleaned every inch of me, she leaves and I sit in the tub until the water is cold.

A thin sliver of roast-chicken smell slides in under the door. Something small moves in my belly.

Hunger.

I dry myself, get dressed and sit at the table. I devour all of the chicken. Mumia and Granny eat mashed potatoes and green beans with the shadow of amused smiles on their lips. When I have eaten all the flesh, I start on the soft little bones. They crunch and crunch under my teeth like satisfyingly stale bread. Each bone is like a stick thrown onto the bonfire of my anger. The gut-punch feeling from earlier has morphed into a good, clean beast. I feed it and feed it. I don't stop until I have eaten the whole chicken, down to the last bit of cartilage, sit back into my chair and burp.

'What's for dessert?' I ask.

*

That night, a heavy rain starts. It drums against my window like the merry strokes of a hammer. I dream of chopping off Shauna's little finger and hammering it onto the fence. Impaled through a purple shellacked fingernail, it twitches.

A Day in Hellford

I wake up from someone ashing their cigarette into my mouth. At least, that's what it feels like. My eyes are glued together, and I pull them apart with my fingers.

Ohhh no.

I've closed my eyes again, but that doesn't alter the fact that the hot, sweaty, heavily breathing body next to me belongs to Dean. I can't stop smelling the alcohol seething from his pores, a musty, bar-carpet smell. The same smell rises from my own arms and face. I decide not to think about it and open my eyes again. Only one is really cooperating. The other is twitching, looking at the back of my head.

It takes more energy than I've actually got to get out of bed, but I do it. I crawl around on all fours to find the top and knickers and leggings I was wearing yesterday, bunched into clammy balls. The room is warped like a singing bowl. I notice an odd itch when I put on my knickers. Next, I have the choice between wearing the leopard-print onesie – from yesterday's jungle party – complete with floor-length tail, or going out in my leggings. It's hella wet and hella cold. It's Hellford that's raining past the window. The glass is all steamed up from our combined alcohol fumes.

The thought of my mother briefly flashes through my mind and I sling the onesie over my arm as though I'm a respectable housewife bringing a prized fur to the dry cleaners. A glimpse at the mirror in the ensuite dispels the illusion. My face is streaked black like a supplicant and there are small animals nesting in my hair. Rustling.

I steal through a bleak trainwreck of a living room: cans, baggies, an apple browned where a bite's been taken out. There's an ashtray where yellowed butts crowd together like there's free stuff to be had. Half of a watermelon on the carpet. A smell like the bottom of the compost bucket.

On weak legs, I make it to the plywood door and push. But the door is not my friend: it has accumulated all the resentment Dean has for me. I picture him on his sticky couch, watching *Football Countdowns*, eating salt-and-vinegar crisps and cursing me under his breath. Crushing empty cans in his big hand, wishing they were my face or my pride, hurling them at the door. I don't understand how you could turn on me like that, the door says, stubbornly refusing to go away, not unlike Dean. Is there somebody else? And finally: do you hate me?

It eventually screeches open (would you ever want to be friends?) and I find myself outside. The daylight hits me like a ton of piss. Still feeling murky, but at least I've taken life into my own hands. I listen for a while but no sound comes from the other side of the resentful door.

Hellford is an accretion of houses that have grown like sores on the lip of a six-lane road. There isn't a time of day or night when you don't hear the sound of cars and it's like a permanent rash on your eardrums. If you were to look at an old-fashioned paper map, where all the yellow lines converge and merge, that's Hellford. There's a special kind of smog in Hellford: its inhabitants never see

130

the sun. After a meek protest in the nineties, the government introduced a scheme to distribute free vitamin D to Hellford residents, accompanied with an insufficiently focus-grouped ad campaign: *We all need the D.*

I take out my phone. It's got ten per cent battery. The thin red line is the last thread connecting me to my normal life. Strange, no messages? I think of work, where I should have been four hours ago. No doubt my unexplained absence is creating quite a stir among the bored call-centre girls. I picture my manager, Laura, excitedly tripping into the HR office for probably the tenth time today. Through the glass walls of the office, the girls see Laura and Tonya putting their heads together like concerned hens, their discussion part genuine concern, part gossip.

'Where do you think she is?'

'It's not like her.'

If I could just call, make it there before the two o'clock team meeting. I try to imagine a scenario where my leopard outfit wouldn't attract any questions. I press the Safari icon over and over again. The irritatingly well-designed writing repeats: Safari cannot open the page because your iPhone is not connected to the internet.

Ohhh Jesus.

I stumble a bit and the passing cars make me queasy to the point of gagging. The air feels lead-heavy with exhaust gas. I clutch my leopard fleece which has already started thirstily sucking in the rain. My own mouth feels parched, but I remember something my mum said once, and keep my mouth closed so as not to take in any Hellford rain. It's as bad for you as drinking petrol, supposedly. My iPhone is my temple, I think, slipping it back into my bra, swatting off acid moths that have started landing all over my naked arms just at the edge of my vision, their dry, brittle wings tickly on my skin. A few rare Hellford inhabitants taking a stroll stop and stare.

Hellford is a one-shop town, and the shop is the An Post office, and that's where I'm headed.

I walk past facades dating back to marginally happier days: in the eighties, the road was only a four-lane, and that's when Halloran's Butcher and Dolly's Cake Accessories must have – not thrived exactly, but not gone under either. Now they are a delicately faded sepia, unified by thousands of layers of fumes. The townspeople's faces are of the same fashionable vintage fade. They look at me as though from underwater, silent. It is said that people here have stopped speaking. They couldn't hear each other over the sound of traffic, anyways. That's not true, of course. At least, I think not.

I make it to the post office. It's got the worst kind of smell for a day like this: warm wet dog with a hint of microwave curry. It's past lunchtime and my brain thoughtlessly suggests that we might eat something. My stomach throws a fit and threatens to jump out of my throat at the thought.

Ohhh Jaysus.

I collapse onto a bench, seeing that all the tellers are busy. There's a sad feeling lurking about this place, poking me in the side and telling me it's the hub of all activity. The smog presses its face against the small windows, FOMO written all over it. Further down, the street erases itself into nothingness.

To distract myself from the bright green, wriggly snakes on the ceiling and the tropical, flesh-eating flowers and the mangroves growing rapidly at the edge of my vision, I observe the tellers. There's a blonde woman in the money window by the door. She seems strangely colourful compared with the other people I've seen here. Two of the tellers in the three general windows are long and lanky glasses-wearing young fellas, their black hair slicked forward with grease and their skin oozing. The third window is occupied by a woman with thick glasses. She has something of a man about her; specifically, Winston Churchill. She sits up straight as an 'I' and her myopic blue eyes are filled with low-key hate. The nausea and knicker itch and soaked leopard onesie are starting to weigh heavy on me, intolerably heavy. I begin to feel somewhat flattened. Part of my elbow has started melting into the bench, and I'm hoping no one will notice. What a mess. My breathing becomes more and more shallow, like there's not enough air. Or, I suddenly think, like my lungs are full of Hellford smog. I casually try to continue inhaling and exhaling, feeling myself turn blue in the face. If I die on this bench, I want it to at least be discreet. I cough up a small, yellow cloud. It hangs there for a second, then disappears. I resume my waiting.

I'm praying I won't get one of the wavering twins, for nausea reasons, but one of their positions opens up. After an exaggeratingly normal volley of looks, which I am hoping will show how absolutely fine I am (me? It's my turn? – looking at the wall behind me, turning back with a now wondrous smile – it's really me? Me? The chosen one?), I approach the window.

'Bus ticket to Galway, please,' I say. In a faraway corner of my being, there's a voice saying: well done, good girl. (That you, Mam? G'way.) The young man watches me with benevolent interest. In fact, as if by magic, all the other positions have freed up and they are all looking at me – friendly but laughing inwardly, I think. He turns to a schedule under the glass top of his desk, runs a finger horizontally then vertically.

'The next bus is ... at five fifteen,' he says, looking pleased.

What? Oh. Nonono. I can't miss a whole day's work without notice. There's a policy for that. In the fireable offence section, if I'm not mistaken. The other, identical-looking teller has slid his hand under his own window, made his arm long like Inspector Gadget and is cleaning the transparent partition next to my face. The insisting squeegee-squeeze is pushing on my brain. I try not to be rude about it but shrink up against the other side.

'What about ... a taxi? Are there taxis? How much would that be?' I ask. A flash of last night in Dean's Audi feels like an ad for not driving and dying. Car black, night black, black road, it was all black. It seemed strangely colourful compared with this place. It's always this way with Dean. Just when I think I've gotten rid of him for good, he wanders back into my life, and I wake up in Hellford, unable to remember how I got here and how to leave.

I crouch and twist to get away from the hand while still getting a partial view of my teller, who helpfully elongates his neck. He is typing something into his browser and slams Enter.

'Taxi would be about a hundred and eighty euro,' he says, apologetically. My belly crumples into itself unhelpfully.

'I'll ... just get the bus ticket, please,' I say in a parched voice. I fish out my phone and remove the cover to get at my emergency cash. I'd rather not think about where I've lost or forgotten my debit card, the one that's got Dean's birthday as a passcode. There are two twenties in my phone and I hold them up in amazement. They are huge and green like ocellated lizards. They are also quite sticky. I wave them in front of my face. Wow. I look back at the guy to share my astonishment. He nods, seemingly impressed. Not bad, huh.

He prints out the ticket from a happy little machine and hands it to me. I sway, suddenly overcome by the nauseating hours in front of me. Should I go outside to wait for the bus? They say Hellfordians cover their bodies in Vaseline when they go out for extended periods of time. I have no idea if that's true or just one of those things my mum made up. But I don't want to find out. My stomach lurches upwards.

'Do you have a bathroom I could use?' I whisper. The teller looks like he's about to say no, then disappears and reappears in the next window, where the woman resembling Winston Churchill sits. He moves his mouth silently and she shakes her head. He tries again and she shoots me a look. Shrugs. The teller comes out the other side:

'You can use the staff bathroom. Here, I'll show you.'

I follow him to a room in the back. It's a mineral-looking and fresh-smelling room, a table and a sink with four neatly aligned cups on the dry rack. A door to the bathroom. Inside it's filthy and ammoniac and I don't even have to try to heave it all out. It's red and the satsuma-sized shapes floating in it look like unhatched baby chicks. I dust off my knees and flush thoughtfully. What happened last night?

When I come out, the Winston Churchill woman is having tea and crackers at the table. Her eyes look like they are small with hate, but she is kind.

'Are you feeling all right, dear?' she asks.

'Food poisoning,' I heave.

'Oh dear. How about a cuppa?'

Her kindness tips me over the edge and I collapse onto the table with my head on my arms and sob. The woman

– who says she is called Margaret – makes my tea milky, without asking. The cup I get has a faded floral pattern. The steam of it cupping my cheek, like Mum used to when she thought I was asleep. Margaret observes me through those glasses that make her eyes small like raisins. She makes conversation but I miss most of it. It seems to be mostly interesting facts from an An Post almanac they stopped producing in the nineties. She seems to be trying to convince me of the usefulness of almanacs.

'For example, do you know why airports are so big?' she says. 'It's to house all the hours lost in them.'

'Always thought it was to do with the size of the planes,' I manage, hoping to contribute to the conversation. She shakes her head pityingly. The two young-fella tellers come in on their break. They stand around with helpless arms and ripe-melon hands swinging. They tell me the bright blonde girl who works the money window is called Jodie, she's from Canada. They're proud of her, I can tell. Proud to have someone come all the way from Canada to live in Hellford. God knows why. Maybe there aren't any pictures of Hellford in Canada. But here she is, with people proud of her. Nobody is proud of me: I broke up with my boyfriend.

'Why did you break up with him then?' Margaret asks.

'Because he didn't know any good blackberry-picking spots,' I say, and a wail follows too close behind to slam the door on it. It lets itself out and shamelessly hurls itself around the room. That bleeding speech therapy always kicks in at the darndest moments. I look at my bitten cuticles to avoid seeing the downcast faces around me.

'Jodie has her own Netflix subscription,' one of the young fellas says softly. I shrink into myself. Could they know I am still using Dean's mum's account? Of course not, I hear my own mum's reasonable-indignant voice say. But something else comes to my mind. I take out my phone and press the round button. The now-humourless screen shows the dead-battery image and goes black again. I ask if anyone has a phone charger, iPhone SE, it's the universal phone one, does anyone have one?

'Jodie has a contact charger, a new type, it only exists in Canada. It's an embalmed human hand. You just put your phone in it, and it is instantly charged.'

I must have misheard. I go up to the front to see Jodie. She smiles brightly and puts my phone on her embalmed hand.

Next, I'm walking up and down the corridor leading from the front office to the staff room. The corridor is lined with shelves full of forms and pamphlets showing happy-faced dolls. How to do this, how to do that. A bold title catches my eye: *How to be normal.* I pull it out and there's a picture of two people in bed, looking a lot like Dean and me, eating Doritos and watching a film, seeming happy. I forget the flier and walk up and down, and believe me, it isn't easy with all the sway on this ship. Well, not ship I guess. I'm trying to get reception in the different spots, but no luck so far. I try taking my shoes off to see if it will make it work any better, remembering something Mum said to us when we were little: wearing rubber boots can prevent you from getting electricity-shocked at the sheep wire. It seems to be a similar situation. The red battery is blinking again.

One of the young tellers observes me for a while.

'There's no data coverage here,' he says. The two young men and Margaret have landlines with really long cables they can bring from their houses. Or maybe he means those portable landlines. It's to do with the smog. I feel sorry but also infuriated. Why did they let me take off my shoes?

'I thought you just wanted to check the time, you know, for your bus,' the young man says apologetically. I look at my phone and decide instead to be friends and panic. It's five fifteen. I run back to my shoes which are sneakers with three sets of laces each. Well, maybe not three. They wriggle like thin white snakes and I am not sure if I should just leave them here and run, but the young man comes over and ties them for me while I cry. I want to say something, but what is it? Instead, I just cough up some more yellow smoke and leave.

I'm running down the toxic road. There's a double-decker bus in the river of red brake lights ahead of me. It's an anonymous white. I have to pace myself to match my academic prowess to my endurance, lungs burning, side stitching. What was it Mum said? Breathe in two, breathe out four, on our runs through forests. We were trying to achieve something; I can't remember what. I run, slowly catching up. But the bus goes through a roundabout and traffic is fluid again – it seems to get away, or did it pull up? Did I see it stop at the bus shelter further up? Is it stalled by traffic again?

I run with all my heart, filling my lungs with Hellford smoke.

Galway Sinking

After ten days, the rains stopped.

We had been holding out in our third-floor flat in spite of helicopters overhead and coastguard boats with loud-speakers. The flooding had started on the second day, and we had watched the slow exodus of cars leaving town. At first, only the Prom and the Claddagh had flooded, which was nothing to write home about. The news showed cars ploughing through knee-high stagnant ocean, with reports of people on the seafront being asked to evacuate as a safety measure. But the waters continued to rise, eating their way up Henry Street, Sea Road and the Crescent, until they reached Salthill Road Lower on the fifth day. We spent much of that day with our foreheads pressed against the cool glass of the balcony door, making occasional trips out onto the balcony to assess the water level. 'It's halfway up the wall at Nile Lodge,' Dean said around midday. His calm never left him and this was what I had liked about him when we first met. Back then, I had felt the urge to bring about some emotion in him, and my efforts had led instead to my falling in love with his handsome, impassive face and brick-like presence. My affections were water off a raincoat, but they pooled in the folds and my miniature reflection I took for reciprocity.

Soon, we didn't need to go outside anymore to see the water level. We had already internalized that water was the enemy, were hunting it down everywhere, even rubbing the sink dry after doing the dishes. Most of the people in our building had left, but we witnessed the rescue of a family on the first floor that had held out. On the ninth and tenth days, brown waters were sloshing up against our balcony from below, carrying dead animals and things too gruesome to mention. At high tide, we had to keep our windows closed and heap old bedding against the door. For once, I was happy our flat faced north, away from the direction of the swell.

'Might be time to bring out the aul canoe,' Dean said with satisfaction.

That damn canoe. It was the whole reason we were still here. Dean's father Lorcán had carved it himself, and for years, it had been taking up space in the spare room. If it hadn't been for the canoe, I could have set up a small area for painting. Not to mention the embarrassment when we had guests: 'So here's your room, make yourself at home – mind the canoe – spare towels on the bow seat.'

Every time I brought it up, Dean had a way of sinking deep into the couch, draping his long legs and arms over the pillows and saying: 'It'll come in handy someday.'

Dean's inertia was his most effective weapon in our by now regular arguments. We used to talk about spending a year out in Australia, leaving behind our customer service jobs, which were always meant to be temporary, for an adventure. We would be poor but sexy. Lately, whenever I reminded him of our plans, he reclined into his passive drape, eyes and face closed: 'One thing at a time,' he said.

I used to think we would join forces to climb out of the rigmarole of meaninglessness we had fallen into after

college, but instead Dean had gotten obsessed with waiting for the next promotion, always just on the horizon. As
for me, I was stuck at the bottom of the ladder: too nega-
tive, they said, at Happy Travel – by which they meant not
corporate enough. I refused to contribute a video of me
playing with the rubber duck they sent in our Feel Good
Flood package. They wanted to post the videos on Instagram, a HR initiative destined to show employees in other
locations, and more importantly, customers, how well they
were taking care of victims of flooding among their staff.

Most of our time during those ten days was spent in
bed. There wasn't much to do apart from look out the
window and forage in the freezer for something edible.
We made love like when we first met: slowly, attentively,
all day long. Joined at the hips, we rocked like Noah's
ark into dreamtime, our surroundings blurry, the world
around slowed to a halt or sped up like a fast-forwarding
videotape, it was hard to tell. On the Velux window, rain-
drops drummed their light blessing. We had the heater
cranked up to five: electricity bills seemed a petty concern
now that the world was going under. These sensual waves
had long held us together. On the window, condensation
from our joint breathing appeared: it was impossible to
tell which drops were his, which mine. By the time we
emerged, we were always surprised to find that it was
time for the next meal.

On the tenth day, the rains stopped and the sudden
absence of their patter was like the death of a familiar pet.
The water level stabilized. At low tide, we could just see
submerged flowerpots one floor below. At high tide, the
water came right up to our flat, the perfect level to climb
over the railing and step into a boat. It had taken the sea ten
days to reclaim the land, but another twenty were needed

until it had flushed out most of the human sediment it had collected on its way in. Day after day, the ebb pulled away like a fishing trawler's net to inventory its catch: the intimate contents of dressers and cupboards, toothbrushes, pillows, kettles, toasters, yoga mats, schools of loose paper, phone chargers, hot water bottles, houseplants, cutlery holders, napkins, wrapping paper, and a few ukuleles. Seemingly disappointed, the flow came back the following morning for more, with the sound of a thousand chairs being dragged across a thousand empty ballrooms, until the waters turned a semi-transparent green. A relentless sun had been shining since the flood, illuminating the sea all the way to the bottom of Salthill Road Lower. Parked cars that hadn't been moved in time wavered eerily underwater, sparking playful glints upwards. They seemed to feel at home down there, at the bottom of the ocean. The high hedge of thuja lining the garden wall on the opposite side of the road had turned into bright green seaweed laundered by the swell. The nozzles at Maxol next door had leaked rainbows at first, but now their hoses undulated like harmless tethered water snakes.

One might have thought the authorities would have come after people holding out, but they had their hands full with evacuees. On the evening news, the Taoiseach explicitly commended the 'courageous men and women' who, through foresight and adaptability and a resilience characteristic of the Irish, had lessened the burden on institutions in favour of the less fortunate. The Taoiseach only exhorted people with health conditions or insufficient survival experience to come forward and be evacuated. Dean laughed dryly: 'Survival experience!'

Lorcán, Dean's father, came and brought tidings from other hold-outers and fresh mackerel. He was delighted with himself. The Carter 34 sailboat he had acquired the previous year to navigate up and down the Shannon now proved to be an excellent investment, contrary to what everyone had predicted. He was used to living holed up in the tiny cabin. The floods had widened his usual play-ground and given him lots of new friends who would finally listen to his long expounded theories on sailing and fishing. I watched from the kitchen as Dean and his father lowered the canoe over the railing. The smell of frying mackerel made my mouth water unreasonably: the past week had been mostly tinned tuna and sweetcorn.

'There we go! Waterborne!' Lorcán exclaimed and smiled at me, revealing his cavern of missing teeth. The few snags he had left were yellow and crooked. You could have planted spuds in the furrows of his wrinkles and his eye-brows were wild forest creatures. Most of what he owned was hemmed with green mould. He was unbanked since the nineties and had his weekly pension rolled up under a damp life vest that doubled as a pillow. You couldn't help but like Lorcán. When I first met him, he had struck me as a lonely old man, his only company a runt named Ratty, crossed more times than the Amazon River. She clawed at the railing, desperate to get onto stable land, making small clanging sounds with her long nails. The poor dog was seasick.

From then on, the canoe was moored to the balcony by a leash long enough to allow for low tide. I imagined the canoe's satisfaction, having waited all these years in a small dry room, finally restored to its element. We would soon get used to the revised order of the doors: what had been the front door on the side of the corridor fell into disrepair and was forgotten, all the comings and goings now con-centrated on the balcony door which opened straight into our living room cum dining room cum kitchen. Instead of living on the third floor, we suddenly lived at street level.

At the end of his ten days of flood leave, Dean set up his laptop in the space left by the canoe and resumed his work as a PayPal customer service advisor. My own travel advisor job on Lower Dominick Street was underwater, so I applied for flood unemployment payment and resigned myself to setting up my easel on the balcony. I finally had time to paint. From the open window, snatches of Dean's voice reached me: *Thank you for calling PayPal help, my name is Dean, who am I speaking with.* The warm weather seemed never to want to end, just as the new ocean outside our windows was obviously here to stay. *Of course I understand, that can be frustrating, how can I help you.* Anyone rowing past moored for a while, stopped for a chat, sometimes accepted a cup of tea and admired my representation of the aluminium sea stretching all the way to the Ferris wheel and the Christ the King church steeple. *Have a lovely afternoon, and if you need any further information, we would be glad to hear from you again.* It was a kind and caring Dean I didn't recognize, but I didn't blame him: I knew from working at the travel agency how all your kindness and patience got exhausted by customers. At the end of the day, we never had much love left to give one another, instead, plenty of pent-up poison.

Lorcán had left us a couple of fishing lines and I cast out mornings before setting up the easel. The fish had started arriving not long after the waters had cleared, lured inland by rich and easy feed. Pollacks had been first, kissing shy noses against windows and streetlamps, circumspect as cats. From above they shone like happy blue leopards, but the first one we reeled in revealed anxious lidless eyes and a sad-smiley face that seemed to have known all along what was in store for it. We stared at it flopping on the floor, silent screams opening and closing its lippy mouth, all its lustre lost, the small body a single muscle.

'There's a Japanese technique where they don't feel anything,' Dean said in a parched voice. 'Just push it straight through the brain.'

I had said I wanted to kill my own fish, a brave survivor's gambit – from now on, I would only eat what I killed – but suddenly I wasn't so sure. I looked at the knife in my hand, until then a friendly kitchen tool connected with carrots and bloodless chicken breast. My hand twitched, thwarted by an invisible wall on the way to the presumed area of the brain. Meanwhile, the fish's screams were getting more and more unbearably silent until I couldn't stand it anymore. I squeezed my head in between couch pillows so as not to hear the inaudible, deafening shouts.

That evening we had it as ceviche and it was delicious, the manner of its death now irrelevant.

After the pollacks, other species followed: freckled cod with repugnant mono-goatees, wrasse clad in light blues and pinks which Lorcán told us to leave alone, slimy plaice with all their features lumped onto the one side, slender dogfish and their hooded, suspicious glares, conger eels always close to street level. Mid-June marked the arrival of schools of clueless salmon from the Killary farms, their cages having been lifted clean out of the seabed during the initial storm. Their stock had been greatly reduced on the short journey from Connemara – by lazy predators as much as by their own inability to find feed. They were bravely and clumsily looking for their own kin; they thought they might belong somewhere up the Corrib, these stateless citizens. The river had turned almost entirely lough but even so, their soft bodies pumped full of antibiotics would never allow them to muscle it upstream. A majority would end up on Galway dinner tables or feed the thriving seagulls. The most discerning anglers refused to haul them in, and Lorcán caught them by hand for Ratty's feed. 'Poor fuckers,' he said, scratching his patchy beard.

Much ink has been caused to flow – some say as much as saltwater – over the economic disparities between the flooded and those who lived above critical level. The well-off on Taylor's Hill Road, inner Salthill residents from mid-Dalysfort upwards and the quiet residential areas north of Barna and Knocknacarra remained inland. But conspiracy theories did not resist closer inspection. Besides, we didn't see what was so bad about living in the sea. Experts discussing corroding buildings and national campaigns to rehome hold-outers had us shaking our heads at the TV. We weren't about to be moved to Mullingar for a few fishes, no sirree. There was talk among hold-outers of making it a permanent thing, a community apart from the rest. No cars, no laws, just the occasional Deliveroo speedboat bringing takeout and hope. It wasn't Australia, but it sure was a new life. I was painting all day and Dean was getting to be a damn good fisherman, even selling the surplus to other hold-outers. He had a smug look on his face these days, as though he had known all along that things would work out his way.

'But what will you do in winter?' my mother asked on the phone, incredulous. Well, what could we do? Crank up the stove and jump in for icy morning swims. Good for the circulation, supposedly.

It was spring by the time my mother finally visited. At that stage, things had deteriorated a bit.

'They're being brainwashed inland,' Lorcán said bleakly, shaking his wise forest-head. We knew: we watched RTÉ too. We were no longer courageous men and women, instead foolish egocentrics who put themselves and first responders at risk.

There had been a couple of drunk-boating accidents. 'No more and no less than inland drink driving,' Lorcán had remarked, which, statistically, was inaccurate. He had a hand in all the hold-out initiatives: the community garden atop Dock Road, the underwater gallery, the nightly bonfire pub on the Harbour Hotel. It was as though he had lived under a rock all these years in preparation for just this event. He blossomed like seagrass.

In spite of it all, I still hoped my mother would understand that we were pioneers, living off the sea, creating a new way of life. My mother had been a pioneer too: in the late seventies, when she was just a young girl, she had taken part in women's marches. Later, she continued going to demonstrations, now a climate change activist. I remembered the one she took us to after the Rio Summit in 1992. I was only six years old at the time and my siblings were not much older. Mother shooed us forward continually, so as not to fall behind among the black flags of the anarchists – how would that look? The next day, in the *Irish Times*, we were among the crowd on the cover page, Mother's red coat well recognisable and our heads shorthanded to small pink pixellated blobs. Mother said we were making social history. My siblings and I did not care much for social history, and I grew resentful towards the organic nut-and-raisin bars I invariably unwrapped in the schoolyard, stealing jealous glances at the other kids' Kinder bars. My mother said Kinder was a manifestation of the devil; privately, I wondered what that said about the other parents. The kid on the packaging had too-white skin and teeth, too-blue eyes, and going forward this was how I pictured the Antichrist. Meanwhile, back home, we were doing three types of recycling – this might sound normal now, but back then, it was embarrassing having friends over.

When I went to college in Dublin, I rebelled by sticking to one bin and microwave meals with as many calories as possible. The distance I had put between my mother and myself had not yet fully resorbed.

Back then, Mother had said I would be grateful one day, and maybe this day had come, I thought, on my way to pick her up. But with each stroke of the paddle bringing me closer to New Dock at the former St Mary's College (now St Mary's fishmarket), doubts grew in my throat. By the time I docked, I had only a thread of voice left to greet her with. She was standing next to a trolley suitcase, primmer than in my memory. Lips hyphenated in pre-emptive disappointment, she watched me secure her suitcase under the yoke.

'Here, Mum, take the stern seat. The stern seat, I said! Are you trying to capsize us?' She was making a great fuss about it, as though she didn't know her left from her right, as though it was an outrage to put an older lady through this.

'Didn't you say you had a motorboat now?'

'Dean is out fishing with the motor.'

She shook her head sorrowfully. 'You look like you've aged ten years. No, you really shouldn't have stayed.' She looked over the edge of the canoe carefully: 'My my, what a lot of sand. It really is true that the ocean floor has reclaimed the streets. On the telly they call it Crab City. Did you know that?'

'We call it Gatlantis,' I said, chest swelling with pride and the pull of the paddle.

Coming up to the flat, I winced at the sight of my paintings laid out on the roof. It was a project encouraged by the underwater gallery crew: pictures of the city post-flood, exposed to the elements of our new environment. Wind, rain, guano. It had even received some interest from forward-thinking inland exhibitions, but I should not have expected my mother to like it.

'Well – do *you* like it?' she asked. 'And what about the *smell*?'

After watching me gut a couple of sea bass with a quick motion I'd thought she would admire, she elected to stay outside, looking nauseated. I had asked Dean to put the bass aside specifically for her, but as she watched their red entrails blossom under her feet, it was clear she wouldn't eat a bite.

'Oh look, there's Lorcán.' She nodded at a nearing boat. I looked up.

'That's Dean, Mum,' I said, shocked. But I could see why she would think he was his father. Same streetlamp stance. Same long rectangular face. He might have folded in a few wrinkles since giving up his job at PayPal to become a fisherman, and there had been a boating accident which had left him missing a tooth. It was such a hassle getting an appointment with inland dentists, we had just forgotten about it. They fretted about our postcode and acted as though we couldn't possibly exist. After the DSP had cut off flood unemployment payments, Ordnance Survey had redefined land boundaries, all part of an effort to convince hold-outers to accept rehoming.

It was pathetic, really, but some of the younger people were giving up and leaving. 'We have our whole lives in front of us,' they said, holding out their palms and spreading their fingers as if to show they weren't webbed. They thought there was a better life for them out there, and there was nothing we could do but watch them walk straight into a lifetime of being call centre fodder. At first, the hold-outers had been a healthy mix of old, visionary art-heads and young, practical people fed up with their nine-to-fives. As the young drained away, only visions remained.

Dean insisted we go to the bonfire pub with Mother as planned. I searched his features, wondering if there was something in the situation I couldn't see which he did. But his face was the usual wall, now illuminated by the flood-lights of a new fanaticism. We loaded the motorboat with a few chairs taken from our neighbours' flats and headed to the Harbour Hotel. The fire was already roaring, and so were the wild men and women sitting and dancing around it. We threw our chairs into the blaze, Mother staunchly refusing to participate, which made Dean go into an offended muteness. I suddenly saw it all through my mother's eyes: these weatherbeaten, emaciated faces and bodies hadn't scared me before, but now they did. My mother seemed frail in comparison. It seemed to me she needed protecting. Fault lines were beginning to appear in the community. Lorcán and the underwater gallery people were pacifists wielding only banjos and uilleann pipes and songs. But there was a group of raucous burners: Barry and his two sons – we only knew them as Cuddy and Big Cuddy – and their friends who made up the majority of the youth. Their eyes were too close together and they all seemed to be part of the same rugby team, one that had mislaid the rules of fair play. The Cuddies arrived late, stayed at the bonfire after everyone had left and pumped loud techno through the biggest loudspeakers they had been able to fish out of the Curry's on Headford Road. The beat was like a second heart in our chests at night, a demented pump like after one too many vodka Red Bulls. Barry and his crew had been looting flats all over the city for electronics which they sold on to dealers camped on the bad side of Bohermore. The money brought with it a trail of loud speedboats, loud women and coke. Barry's men were angry and righteous, they felt abandoned by the government, they claimed that they took what they needed to take, it was all covered by people's insurance anyways. Some of the former inhabitants had awoken to a spring nostalgia and came to visit their old flats, only to find them violated by Barry's men. There were court cases starting and it didn't reflect too well on us. Barry's men were complaining that there was nothing left to take, now that so many houses had been sealed. They laid long hard stares on the players with their instruments.

After coming home, I lay awake for a long time, worried about the beat that must have been keeping my mother awake. I tried to talk to Dean about my worries, but he mumbled something about intolerance and sank into sleep like a stone into water. I touched his back but it shivered and rejected me: the body was master of the ship now, the mind no longer in control. He walked the fields of dreams alone and I could feel him getting away from me, night after night, to wake up each morning a little more feral.

My mother left the following day, having refused to use the bathroom even once because of the frogs.

When they cut off the electricity, that didn't make things any easier. Most of us had switched to wood stoves, but still. When they shut off the freshwater supply, that certainly didn't make things any easier. Lorcán set up a rainwater tank for us. Something had stopped them from taking these actions before, some human rights law. But now there was no law, just hope in dwindling amounts. And when Barry's crew started looting the houses of hold-outers, that didn't make things easier for anyone either. Most people left, then.

'*They* did this to us.' After dark, Dean lay awake peering out at the street-river through a crack in the curtains, looking for the light from Woodie's bamboo torches caressing the waves – looters looking for accessible homes. How could a community of a hundred hopeful souls have turned into this archaic dichotomy of cops and robbers? Our nights became Swiss cheese. We were at best half-asleep, at worst half-awake. We had sex with the energy of despair, trying to create a spark through mere friction, but it was useless, like rubbing two pieces of wet wood together. Even though it was summer again, the clammy cold made taking our clothes off an unpleasant experience. Eventually we kept the top on, transformed into a hybrid half-jumper, half-genitalia creature joined at the hips. Instead of dreamtime, I had moments of unpleasant lucidity, eyes suddenly focusing on the shelf above our bed, the uneven traces of paint on the wall.

Inside me, Dean felt cold and metallic like a speculum. His release was a death rattle. 'Who are you?' I wanted to ask, turning around to his closed face. But he was as far away as if he was sleeping.

It wasn't long before Dean and Lorcán started sitting up all night with hurleys on the table, spinning reminiscences of a much better recent past into dawn. It was rumoured that they might be sending in the army to arrest us all. There was no doubt in my mind that it had all gone too far, but whenever I walked into the living room to talk about changing our situation, father and son had the same caveman gleam in their pairs of identical eyes, the same quick neck-jerk of men who had always wanted to be a bit more like animals. I was a small girl again, interrupting a boys' game: I didn't get it. One evening, after I went to bed, I texted my mother saying I was ready to come home.

At daybreak, I tiptoed through the living room where they had laid their identical faces onto forearms and fallen asleep. I climbed over the banister and unmoored the canoe. Small friendly waves were making early-morning songs against the gunwales. The sun was gliding up the church steeple like a disco ball, turning the sea into a glittering dance floor. Small clouds of hope were getting stuck on pointy roofs and chimneys. It was beautiful and I paused for a long time, letting rays trickle down from my frozen scalp onto my chin, then I pushed myself off the balcony. I buried the blade and cut through golden syrup, heading for New Dock. My mother's car was parked by the bleary-eyed fishmarket. When she saw me she came out and stood there, shivering and hugging herself. Swans lay on the water above the green like aquatic sheep, necks asleep under wings, and they didn't stir when I docked. I walked on the loud, uneven planks without looking back, a Eurydice with no need for an oaf of an Orpheus.

I had thought it out, knew someone who worked for Apple who would refer me. I would suck it up and go back to phone calls and live chats, just until I got back on my feet, or maybe after a while there could be a progression – I could become that middle manager cheerfully telling people that things would get better in a month's time. I could get a room overlooking an unwavering street, a normal life. Dean might follow eventually and get his old job back. That's the good thing about these big companies: they're so devoid of human feeling that they never hold a grudge, only see that you're already trained up and take you back and grind you down under the thumb of your utter replaceability all over again. My mother didn't hug me although I could tell she wanted to. I looked down at the dull grey earth, solid and fishless, a ground to walk on, because that's what people do.

When They Cut Me Open

At the end there was water
before that a life, not much of a life
I only wish I'd known a man's touch (though some of the
sisters say it isn't all it's cracked up to be)
not much of a life, no, compared to the brown transparency
of water at first then opaque and opaquer as strand by
strand
spring after spring the safe-underfoot-reeds laid
themselves across my face like the crosses my sisters and
I used to braid.
At first, there was a slow-life-lake – the holy man's assistant
cut my life vessels loose as if I were a goat or a horse no
quiver led his knife astray his gaze did not linger on my
mossy mound any more than it would have lingered
on the soft belly of a goat or a horse
unmoved by the thought that his was the first gaze on my
young thighs and the cut was the same too as though we
all had the same life vessels in our bellies
as though the dog the goat and the horse sacrificed before
me were all members of a family I belonged to also and I
grasped at the last moment that this was true
and had been known by the holy man's assistant for some
time and that it was one of the secrets passed down from

155

mouth to ear and mouth to ear in this – our – tradition of greatness of memories that are never lost
always passed down
and that this was why the shamans bade us never harm an animal if we could help it. My mouth half opened to blurt out the secret but already it was filling with decay-lake-water and it occurred to me that mother had told us
don't drink decay-lake-water only spring-water girls or dug-water girls not all water is the same girls
but this is a silly concern when you're sinking fast weighed down by fourteen golden torcs on your arms and neck and legs into a lake that is quickly colouring winter-thorn-fruit-red from your life vessels bursting out of your belly like they'd thought of nothing else your whole life unravelling in watery silence but slow
as though sun-passage itself had stilled and my last living thought was one of joy for in the energetic red in the elegant unfurling the shamans would read
a happy harvest and few storms for winter.
Decay-lake-water filled my mouth filled my whole body it seemed quickly replacing the blood I had now offered to the slow-life-lake or the gods
I didn't understand it all they hadn't deemed it necessary to explain
seeing as I was going away so soon
my mother didn't cry but rubbed my body with the good butter and four men had to carry me because the weight of the torcs was too much for me to even lift my head.

At the end there was water
brown-red then sunset-pink and finally brown again then black with a white drop of moon and the chants dimmed and went away. I was left alone in silence on a bed of reeds

half gone-to-earth
preserved relics from another spring like me and I knew
that my rest would be eternal safe-underfoot-reed layered
atop safe-underfoot-reed
crisscross crisscross
like the symbols we used to hang above the door against
fire and more and more until they covered me and I
remained in the dark, spring after spring came to rest on
me until the whole slow-life-lake was filled
and wasn't a lake anymore instead a spongy thriving
colony of stalky-greens and bird-feed-flies. A soft layer
of sleeping-moss covered my burial mound like once
the moss between my legs had covered the birth-mound
which had elicited so few comments from the men at my
funeral
though perhaps some had passed between them later after
they had drink taken, away from the holy lake. And I felt
holy and I felt we were whole
I felt the slow mutation of big-grandmother
spring after spring and harvest after good harvest, perhaps
I liked to think, perhaps they were good thanks to me
and it pleased me to have my life's blood soaked up into
the soil growing into thin-green-stalks and later into
strong-gold-oats to feed the beasts and men who stomped
over my old ground.
Was it warm where I was?
Maybe it was, maybe it was warm and humid, glistening
darkly, brown and spongy filaments of earth spun around
my body like I myself was a life vessel in another big body.

But soon – much too soon! – there came an unwelcome
light – and with what
brutality –

I hadn't known such
violence
since the shaman's assistant had slit open my carrying-
promise – a metal spade hacking with unholy repetition
clanged against a torc on my arm and
cut my arm right off
with its next bite. And it was as if sun-passage, instead of
continuing at its greatly slowed-down pace, stopped and
began spooling backwards a bad mad sign the holy people
warned us of a time when salmon-rivers would flow
uphill
and black-summer-birds would fall out of the sky like
stones
and this seemed to be happening now the safe-underfoot-
reeds that were gently solidifying on top of my face were
moved when they shouldn't have been moved, bright
light flooded my body and I heard once more the excited
chants of men. A gloved hand grabbed
my decapitated arm
and tore it out of its resting place tore it right out yes of
the good black peat and held it up like a war-axe limp it
was from dissolved inner-branches held it up against the
shouts of men always men taking my body as a thing to
be torn apart at their will they were shouting for my body
but also for my bangles. One of them shouted a word that
could only mean: 'Gold! Gold!' – in every age this word
always rings the same in
the mouths of men
no matter the syllables I'd heard it from the gullets of my
brothers and the tribe's warriors, to the men loot meant
gold but to the women it meant blood it meant the washing
off of flesh and
rust-coloured love

that clung to a taken piece of gold as stubbornly as its original owner and let me tell you that it put the women right off gold the women whose hands were cold in red water while the men built higher and higher fires forgot the blood and
remembered only the gold.
It hurt when they cut open my carrying-promise and it hurt when they cut off my arm yes you can laugh but it did, the beast with spades for teeth ripped it off and it hurt, it hurt very much.

Though I was then excavated handled and transported with all the exquisite deference normally afforded to a person of my rank – I a king's daughter – nothing assuaged my anger my great quiet invisible anger at being thus ripped out unripe of the peat-body that had grown around me had unbirthed me and become my promise-mother and the great black slash across the belly of the earth looked like my own scar like these men were sacrificing the whole land only I wondered where they would find a holy lake big enough to drown it in and
my torn-off arm with one bangle missing
was laid out next to me in the transport which was closed-off fast and white and this annoyed me more than anything or maybe it was the faces of men – though there were women too –
the faces of men who looked like they knew what they were doing
who thought they'd seen the likes of me before who compared me to the find of an elk or vase not knowing the last thing about me speculating about the violence of my death
some with impudence suggesting that I might have been

an adultress – I, a thousands-of-springs virgin! – others
guessing at war sacrifice suicide. And though only gloved
hands touched me they hurt
yes laugh away if you want
they hurt me I who had been touched only gently by safe-
underfoot-reeds yes this speechless boneless eyeless lump
felt anger rage pain and I cursed yes cursed each hand that
grabbed at my leathery flesh.

Instead of interrogating my innards my teeth or my hair by
burning them or throwing them into water in the normal
way
they prodded with sharp metal
they weighed and illuminated turned me this way and that
on a table as cold as the inside of an oyster they removed
all my heavy gold and took it away to be cleaned before
sliding it painfully back onto my limbs for display
as though it hadn't altered in all these springs
and those raging imbeciles never even copped that one of
the torcs had gone missing instead musing on the spiritual
significance of the number thirteen
I knew the man who had taken it the peat-cutter with the
thick yellow nails
all my curses were on his head I grew tired of distributing
so many curses
more than all the executions I had ordered as my father's
daughter more than all the horses ridden to death on my
behalf more than all the wild cats I had impaled when their
screeches kept me up at night. The stories of the shamans
had come true – we had always listened to their stories like
a tribe of children not believing they could come to pass
not really – but here they were
the naked clouds

no shading-tree-canopies no swarms of flower-travel-flies bird-feed-flies overpopulate-flies no angler-birds stalking-birds good-to-eat-birds or sky-and-oat-songbirds everything that had lived and buzzed around us had been turned into cold solids the collective din of which would have deafened any hunter to the soft paws of prey.

There remained the smallest flocks of forlorn birds a handful of earth creatures grown subdued and shy puddles of forest and water just enough for basic rituals and I wondered at how far some of the people must have to go

to give the earth and roots the thanks they are due at each sunrise. The shamans had said that when the birds started falling out of the sky the sea would soon rise again like it had risen before:

the water had become mountains and crashed down as fast as a woodpecker's beak and where there had been people there was only the deep blue sea

one day they said the sea will rise again but this time we'll know we'll flee inland and build boats, we won't trust the sea's sly promise of a slow progress this time a slow rise that a tribe can adapt to by moving inland every spring, there won't be another mass watery grave. So it surprised me to see these foolish people's ramshackle constructions too close to a dangerous coast the sea was still preaching a reassuring ebb and

flow predictable as sun-passage but I could feel her seething I could feel her gathering herself up like a big cat for the jump somewhere in her black depth where no people lived she was breathing in dilating herself to rise up once more and do away with whole tribes in one bite of her big soft mouth

but   where   were   the   shamans?

For many sun-passages it did not occur to me that the shamans had gone as extinct as the birds and flies. The stories must still be there though must still be alive in some vessel other than the leathery mummy that I was so I interrogated the women. At all times when the stories had been at risk of dying when all the men had been killed the stories continued to live quietly inside of women who passed them on between themselves almost without words until the day one of the boys they bore picked up the stories and claimed them for the menfolk again and declared them holy and the women unworthy of them and the women meekly surrendered but never forgot the old stories –
but these women here wore gloves and white garments as if for a sacrifice or a wedding and handled their small weapons and were far away – unlistening. Their small monthly bleeds were laughable compared with the glorious blaze of my last blood. I interrogated the men but found only shame where holiness should be
only knowledge where there should have been wisdom.

My spirit had clung to my body for so long – in the bog, things are conserved that should never be lost – and it died on this white table it escaped like smoke and became part of
the spirit of all things.

Acknowledgements

Thank you faithful friends who read my work with care and attention, Anne, Sarah and Laure. Faraway friends Sonia, Anne-Claire, Louise and Alice, thank you. Thank you to my family for supporting my writing endeavours. Thank you to the editors of magazines that platformed me, especially John Patrick McHugh at *Banshee* and Claire Healy at *Profiles*. Thank you to Eimear Ryan for editing this work with a gentle but sure touch. For sharing your work with me, talented writers Sinéad, Arthur, Paul, Jord, and others, thank you. Thank you to Mike McCormack and my fiction class at the University of Galway for taking my writing seriously, and to Liz Quirke for waking up the poetry in me. Thank you to my writing-swimming goddess Katharine, for making me come away energised and confident from each dip at Blackrock. A big thank you to Lisa for being the best boss a writer could ask for. Thank you to the Arts Council for granting me an Agility Award in 2022, enabling me to finish this work, and again in 2024, for my next adventure.

More than anything, thank you Hélène, my albatross, the Louise to my Thelma, not just for being my first reader, and not just for your excellent taste which shaped

me and my writing; but for making me see beauty in
dark times, and for letting in the light.